Praise for *Fatal Forgery*

"I loved the sense of place, with some surprising revelations about jail and courthouse conditions and operations, and an interesting change of setting at one point, which I won't reveal for fear of spoiling the plot. There was great attention to detail woven skilfully into the writing, so I felt I learned a lot about the era by osmosis, rather than having it thrust upon me. All in all, a remarkable debut novel."
Debbie Young, author and book blogger, UK Ambassador for the Alliance of Independent Authors

"From the start of this story I felt as if I had been transported back in time to Regency London. Walking in Sam's footsteps, I could hear the same cacophony of sound, shared the same sense of disbelief at Fauntleroy's modus operandi, and hung onto Constable Plank's coat tails as he entered the squalid house of correction at Coldbath Fields. I am reassured that this is not the last we shall see of Samuel Plank. His steadfastness is so congenial that to spend time in his company in future books is a treat worth savouring."
Jo at Jaffareadstoo, Amazon 'Top 500 Reviewer"

Praise for *The Man in the Canary Waistcoat*

"Having read the first Sam Plank novel and really enjoyed it I was so looking forward to the next, and 'The Man in the Canary Waistcoat' did not disappoint. Susan Grossey is an excellent storyteller. The descriptions of Regency London are vivid and create a real sense of time and place. Sam Plank, Martha and Wilson are great characters – well-drawn and totally individual in their creation. The dialogue is believable and the pace well fitted to this genre. The novel shows excellent research and writing ability – a recommended read."
Barbara Goldie, The Kindle Book Review

"Regency police constable Sam Plank, so well established in the first book, continues to develop here, with an interesting back story emerging about his boyhood, which shapes his attitude to crime as an adult. Like the first book, this is not so much a whodunit as a whydunit, and Grossey skilfully unfolds a complex tale of financial crime and corruption. Another feature that really lifts this series for me is the underlying compassion and humanity of the characters, and there are fascinating details about daily life in the criminal world woven into the story, leaving the reader much more knowledgeable without feeling that he's had a history lesson."
Debbie Young, author and book blogger, UK Ambassador for the Alliance of Independent Authors

WORM IN THE BLOSSOM

Susan Grossey

Susan Grossey
Publisher

For my grandmother Edna,
who always believed that every single word
I wrote was marvellous

Who will guard the guards themselves?

—JUVENAL

Author s note

Any period of history has its own vocabulary, both standard and slang. The Regency was no different, and in order to capture the spirit of the time I have used words and phrases that may not be familiar to the modern reader. At the end of this book there is a glossary of these terms and their brief definitions.

CHAPTER ONE

An unexpected visitor

TUESDAY 18TH APRIL 1826

I thought it was a cat at first. Just as you turn into Norton Street there is a yard on the corner, used by a local blacksmith during the day. At night he pulls an old wooden door across the entrance to keep out the curious, and as I walked past it I heard a high-pitched whimper. Martha's never that keen when I bring home stray animals, as she says – with some justification – that as soon as you get fond of them, they find their feet and leave you, but I had a look anyway, expecting to see a mother cat and some kittens. Instead, as I inched the door to one side and peered through the fog into the yard, two very human eyes looked back at me from the shadows.

"Now then, who are you?" I asked. "Come on, lad – you shouldn't be in here." I pushed the door aside and stepped into the yard.

"I'm not a lad," replied the girl with some difficulty, drawing in a breath between each word. "And I want my ma!" With the last word came that whimper again. Her hand shot out and grabbed hold of mine with unexpected ferocity. "Please, mister – get my ma!"

"Does she live near here?" I asked.

The girl screwed her eyes shut and shook her head. Again, that awful mewl, and I made up my mind.

"Well, I do," I said, "and my wife's at home and will know what to do." I bent down to the girl. "Here: put your arm around my neck, and I'll pick you up." She looked at me with uncertainty. "I'm a constable – I look after people." Another whimper, and I scooped her up before she could object. She was heavier than I expected, and by the time I reached home and kicked the door to summon Martha, I was sweating.

Martha took one look at us and realised in an instant what I had missed. As I stood in the kitchen, the girl unprotesting in my arms, my wife whirled around us, making preparations and issuing instructions.

"Keep hold of her for a moment while I get the spare bedspread from the cupboard. Now, bring her through here and put her down – no, not on the chair, here on the floor. That's it: put the cushions around her. No, don't light the fire – she'll be too hot with that. But you can bank up the range, and fill the two large pots with water and put them to heat."

All the while she was making little shushing noises to the girl – not words, exactly, but just sounds of comfort and presence.

"Now, Sam, you'll have to go out. Back to the police office is probably best, and then I'll send word when you can come home. And on your way past, knock for old Sadie and ask her to come with her birthing bag." And with a quick peck on the cheek, I found myself once again outside.

CHAPTER TWO

Little Martha

WEDNESDAY 19TH APRIL 1826

At about six the next morning, Thomas Neale the office-keeper nudged me awake. I rolled my neck and stretched my arms above my head; it was not the first night I had spent on that bench in the back room of Great Marlborough Street, but it never seemed to grow any softer.

"Your Martha's sent word that you can go home now," Tom said, handing me a cup of tea. "You must have really upset her this time. Fine woman, too – if she grows sick of your antics, you know where to send her." He winked: I knew that in my choice of wife I was the envy of many men of my acquaintance.

I shook my head. "No, nothing like that. We had an unexpected visitor – well, two – and she wanted me out of the way." I put on my coat and yawned widely. "I'll be good for nothing today, Tom. Can another man take my hours?"

Tom nodded. "I thought you'd say as much. I've checked the roster and sent a lad round for Constable Wilson. He'd walk through fire for you, let alone cover your hours."

When I reached home there was already the smell of baking in the air, so I knew that all was well. Martha was sitting at the kitchen table, pouring a cup of tea for the handywoman, and the two of them glanced frequently at the blanket-lined dresser drawer resting on the table next to them. Fast sleep in the middle of its woollen nest, chubby fists curled on its chest like a squirrel, was a baby.

"Meet little Martha," said my wife. "Named after me."

The handywoman sniffed. "When you've delivered as many babies as I have, dear, the novelty wears off. There are more Sadies in this street and the next than you can shake a stick at." Like me, she saw Martha's smile falter and reached across to pat her hand. "But the first – you're right: that is something special. Here's to little Martha – after a start like that, things can only improve for her." And she raised her cup and drained it in salute. "And now I must be off. I'm not as young as I used to be, and Mrs Darwin above the butcher's is just about ready with her fourth." Martha handed her her bag. The old woman stood for a moment, contemplating my wife. "You've a good touch, Martha Plank. Good instincts. Not many have, even those who've had their own."

Martha nodded wordlessly.

After a few hours' sleep, I woke in the early afternoon and went down to the kitchen. Sitting near the range was the new mother, and I looked away quickly when I realised she was feeding her child. Martha smiled reassuringly at her, and adjusted the shawl that was draped around the girl to cover the baby and the breast.

"This is Mr Plank, Alice – my husband. He's the one who found you and brought you here."

Alice nodded but said nothing. She didn't meet my eye. Martha squeezed her shoulder. "He's a good man, Alice. Not one to frighten you." Alice nodded again, and this time glanced shyly up at me. I smiled in what I hoped was a good way.

"You've a pretty little girl there, Alice," I said. "One of the prettiest I've seen, I should say." The new mother beamed broadly at this, for who can resist praise of their child? "Now Martha – or should I say, my Martha – could you come upstairs and help me find a fresh shirt?"

In the bedroom I pushed the door to and sat on the edge of the bed, pulling Martha down next to me. "Alice," I said.

"Alice Godfrey," said Martha. "She told Sadie."

"Have you taken a good look at her?" I asked. Martha nodded. "How old do you think she is?"

Martha looked down at her hands. "She told us she's fourteen."

"Did Sadie say anything about her physical condition?"

"Only that she was very, well, unformed. Really only a child."

"Was there any mention of the father?" Martha shook her head. "Violation?" My wife bit her lip and looked up at me. I took her hand. "If a man has forced himself on her, there may be something we can do – at least have him acknowledge the child and pay towards its upkeep."

"It may be difficult for Alice to say precisely who..." started Martha. "I'll show you what I mean. Wait here."

A few minutes later Martha came back into the bedroom with a bundle of clothes. "This is what Alice was wearing. I will launder it all for her, of course, but look." She nudged me off the bed and set about laying out the clothes as though displaying them in a haberdashery. Once she had finished creating a flat and dismembered person there on our bed, she stood back with her hands on her hips and waited for me to say something. "Well?"

I leaned forward and took stock. "The neckline is very low cut," I said. "Much more revealing than any you would wear." Martha sniffed. "And the skirt," I felt the fabric, "is of quite fine stuff."

"And has been turned up, to show these." Martha indicated the adjusted hem of the skirt with one hand, and the pair of stockings with another. "Look at that embroidery. You know how dear are clocked stockings. Not silk, to be sure, but fine all the same. Now where would a young girl like Alice get the money for such stockings – or why would someone pay for them for her?"

"You think Alice has a patron?" I mused.

Once again, my sensible wife surprised me. "No patron would have allowed a pregnancy to continue to this stage, or he would have hidden her away in the country to have her baby. I don't think she has a patron: I think she has an abbess." She smiled at the look on my face. "And as you know several such women of commerce, Samuel Plank, I suggest you ask some questions." She started folding up Alice's clothes, and as she did so a strong scent filled the room. I caught her arm.

"Wait, Martha – can you smell that? Is it coming from the clothes?"

We both bent towards the bed and sniffed. Martha wrinkled her nose. "I did notice that earlier, but thought it might be something in Sadie's bag of potions. But it's on the clothes."

"And it's not herbal or medicated," I said. "That's something scented."

Martha held up the items one by one. On the chemise there was a dark stain, greasy to the touch. I took the garment from her to smell it. Martha looked enquiringly at me.

"Scented pomade, I should imagine," I said.

"For gentlemen's hair?"

I nodded.

"From a gentleman visitor?" she suggested. "Perhaps he bent his head to kiss her..." She indicated her own bust.

"Perhaps," I agreed. Just then a loud wail floated up towards us. "And we'll have to see about where to take Alice for safekeeping – I'm not sure I'm up to having two Marthas in the house, calling for attention."

CHAPTER THREE

The house on Harrison Street

FRIDAY 21ST APRIL 1826

Martha was right: there was someone I could ask about Alice's situation, and at the end of that week I went to see her. It had been several months since I had called on Mrs Eliza Welcome – or the Warmest Welcome, as her gentleman visitors knew her. As with many of her profession, the married title was purely honorary. She had come to London, like hundreds before and since, looking for her fortune – and, like so many of them, she quickly found that she had only one thing to sell. Starting out as a barque of frailty, she was lucky: as her beauty faded her business acumen increased. She navigated carefully through the choppy waters of sin, avoiding the twin dangers of pox and gin, and before long she was running her own group of lightskirts. Thanks to some timely investment advice from a grateful customer who worked at the Bank of England, she was able to set up in some style, and it was to this Golden Square mansion – known as the Aviary, as it was home to so many birds of paradise – that I turned my steps now.

I gave my name to the maid at the door, and was shown into a small waiting room and then ushered into Mrs Welcome's private parlour.

"Constable Plank," she said smoothly, inclining her head. "A delight." She indicated the plump velvet armchair alongside her own and I sat.

"I trust I find you in good health, Mrs Welcome, this fine spring day."

"You do, constable, you do. May I?" She lifted a teapot from the tray beside her and poured me a cup. "Mr Twining may be trying his hand at banking these days, but I prefer his tea." We both sipped companionably for a couple of minutes until the striking of the mantel clock seemed to remind her that constables rarely make social visits. "And so how may I be of assistance to you today, constable?" she asked. Mrs Welcome knew full well that the judicious supply of information to constables like me was part of the price she had to pay to be allowed to continue her business relatively undisturbed.

"My wife and I have a young girl in our care. I found her by chance, about to have her baby in the street like a dog." Mrs Welcome shook her head sadly but said nothing. "When my wife talked to her – Alice Godfrey, she's called – and examined her and her clothing, it became clear that she is..." I waved my hand to indicate the premises around me.

"A prostitute, constable?" enquired Mrs Welcome sweetly.

"Indeed."

"But I have no Alice – Godfrey, you say? – working for me, Constable Plank."

"Oh no, she is not one of your girls – that is immediately apparent. Alice is only fourteen."

"Fourteen? And if she has had a baby, then conception was perhaps when she was thirteen?"

"Quite possibly, yes." I put down my cup and leaned towards the abbess. "Mrs Welcome, I know that within these walls you cater for a variety of tastes and preferences. But you do not, I believe, sell children."

Mrs Welcome reared back in her seat. "I most certainly do not, sir – most definitely not. My ladies are all of an age to choose their own profession."

"But there are some abbesses who are less scrupulous..." I let the half-question hang.

She inclined her head slightly. "There are men who prefer their encounters to be – pure. To meet this need,

there are certain deceptions that a woman can employ."
She paused. "And so some men will seek an absolute
guarantee of purity by insisting on a very young woman."
I raised my eyebrow. "A child, yes."

"And you know where such purity can be found?"

Mrs Welcome gnawed her lip as she considered.

"Of course, it might be prudent for me to satisfy myself that no such children are indeed on the premises by a
thorough search of all the rooms," I suggested, making as
though to stand.

"You might pay a visit to a lodging house in Harrison
Street. The landlady is a Mrs Marwood – known to many
as Mother Marwood."

Harrison Street leads off Gray's Inn Lane in Bloomsbury,
and I knew the area mainly for the Foundling Hospital,
an imposing building a couple of streets south of my destination. Just coming out of Harrison Street as I arrived
was a rabbit-seller, his pole across his shoulder and a few
rabbits still swinging from it, and I asked him which was
the lodging house of Mrs Marwood.

"Corner o' Frances Street. The lady of the house is
home now, and looking forward to a delicious rabbit
stew." He raised his hat to me and headed off in search of
more hungry housewives.

The house he had identified was a three-storey dwell-
ing, hugging neighbours on both sides but with a good,

airy aspect from its corner position. I knocked and heard reluctant footsteps stomping towards me before the door was hauled open. A grubby-looking maid of all work glared at me.

"Well?" she said. "I haven't all day, you know. Some of us have work to do." I daresay that had I been wearing my uniform she would have been a deal more civil, but if I want to be taken for a man in the street, I have to be prepared to be treated as one.

"I'd like to see Mrs Marwood. About one of her girls."

The maid sniffed and rubbed her sleeve across her nose. She looked appraisingly at me, and after a few moments she jerked her head over her shoulder. "Wait in there, and I'll get her."

The parlour of the house was pleasantly light, with windows giving out in two directions. The walls were painted a fashionable – but to my eye bilious – shade of yellow, and a large portrait of a man stared severely down on me from above the mantelpiece. A bureau was open in the corner of the room, papers spilling out of it, and I had to restrain myself from going over to look at them. An armchair was drawn close to the fireplace, while a more upright pair of chairs and a small drop-leaf table stood by one of the windows. There was a small pile of books on the table, and I contented myself with leafing through one of these while I waited.

After about ten minutes the parlour door was pushed open and in came Mrs Marwood. Younger than I had expected, she wore a blue afternoon dress with a white chemisette, and – from the way she kept putting her hand to her hair – I suspected that she had only just changed. She smiled at me and indicated one of the two chairs by the window.

"Delighted to meet you, Mr...?" she began in a voice that tried hard to sound genteel but struggled to hide all traces of a more humble beginning.

"Plank," I supplied. "Mr Samuel Plank." I bowed and took the chair. She sat opposite me.

"I understand from Matthews that you are interested in one of my resident young ladies."

I nodded. "I am indeed. One in particular has been spoken of – Alice, I believe her name is. Alice Godfrey." I was not at all sure that this was where Alice had been so misused, but Mrs Marwood's reaction was all I needed. Her welcoming smile faltered for a moment, and she re-adjusted her features into an expression of regret.

"Ah, what a shame, Mr Plank," she said. "Alice is indeed a charming young woman, but sadly indisposed at the moment. Might I interest you in the company of another of our residents? They all have special qualities. Is there something in particular that you seek?" She smiled sweetly again, cocking her head to one side in a manner she no doubt thought both inviting and comforting. "A specific appetite you wish to sate?"

"Mrs Marwood," I replied, clearing my throat as though with nerves, "Mrs Marwood, I am a man who has travelled widely and sampled much. And I find myself jaded. Weary, if you will." My hostess nodded sympathetically. "Modern women are too, let us say, knowing for my taste – their sophistication dampens my interest. I prefer a more unspoilt experience." I paused and looked straight at her and enunciated the next two words very clearly. "Totally unspoilt."

Mrs Marwood raised a delicate hand to stop me. "You need say no more, Mr Plank. Alice, alas, is of no use to you any longer – you will understand that there are other gentlemen who also prefer the company of such stainless creatures. But if you are willing to bide your time a little, I am sure I can find you the perfect companion. Would you care to leave an address, or...?"

I shook my head; I doubt many who visited Mrs Marwood would be foolish enough to give their true details.

"Now that I know that you will be able to provide what I need, madam, I shall call again in, shall we say, a fortnight? And in the meantime you can keep an eye out for a young lady who might suit my needs."

Mrs Marwood inclined her head in agreement and held out her hand. I pressed it to my lips and, with supreme self-control, did not retch.

CHAPTER FOUR

Two wild horsemen

MONDAY 24TH APRIL 1826

The following Monday I went about my duties, all the while considering what to do about Mother Marwood and her vile trade. When I called in at Great Marlborough Street to see if there were any afternoon warrants, I found that Conant had left a message for me to attend him in his dining-room at four, and at five minutes to the hour I made my way upstairs. He was tending to some papers, so he waved me to a chair.

In all walks of life you will find the diligent and the lazy, the curious and the unquestioning. This is certainly true in my own line of work, and on many occasions, while listening to the tales told by fellow constables, I have thanked whatever providence brought John Conant and me to Great Marlborough Street at the same time.

19

Although we are both bound, of course, to work with whomever is on duty – he with other constables and I with other magistrates – we both, I believe, feel that it is in our particular partnership that we gain the greatest satisfaction and make the most important discoveries.

The clock on the mantelpiece chimed, and a few moments later the footman brought a young lad of about sixteen into the room. Conant beckoned the boy forward.

"You are Croft?" he asked, and the lad nodded. He was a well-formed boy, his clothes tidy and of the right size – I guessed him to be in service, living in, with access to good food. "Croft here is a groom in Sir John Brigstock's household. This morning the coachman there, a…" Conant looked down at a piece of paper, "a George Parker, came to see me about something that Croft had noticed. We would like to hear about it from you, Croft." The magistrate took off his glasses and smiled encouragingly at the groom.

"Well, Your Lordship, I mean, Your Majesty, no, not Your Majesty." The groom turned red with his efforts.

"Mr Conant is a magistrate, and I am a constable," I said, "and you can call us both sir."

The groom swallowed. "Thank you, sir." We all waited. "Oh yes, what I saw. Sir John has two sons, well, had two sons." I noticed the correction but said nothing. "Mr Edward is the older, and Mr Francis the younger. Three days ago they went out riding together, to Rotten

Row. They both like riding fast, and Mr Edward often challenges his brother to races. I prepared their horses – Beacon for Mr Edward and General for Mr Francis. And then there was the accident." He stared down at his hands.

"Francis Brigstock was thrown from his horse," explained the magistrate. "He hit his head and was killed outright. The only person who saw it happen was his brother. They were galloping through the park – not along Rotten Row – and no-one else was about."

"But it's the horse, sir, Mr Francis's horse, General," said Croft in anguish. "They talk of destroying him, saying he's unreliable and a bolter. But he's not, sir. He's the steadiest of mounts. And when I was rubbing him down afterwards, I noticed something. There was a deep mark across his rump – from a crop." I must have looked puzzled. "Oh, I know Mr Francis had a crop, of course, sir, but it's the angle of the mark – it couldn't have come from his own rider. And it must have been a hard whack to leave such a mark. Poor General, sir – I think he was hit by someone else and took fright."

"And the only person who could have done it was Mr Edward Brigstock," I said.

Croft looked down at his hands again and said nothing.

Once Croft had left, the magistrate turned to me.

"Well, Sam?" he asked.

"Inheritance, perhaps?" I suggested.

Conant shook his head. "Unlikely; a motive for a younger son to kill an older, maybe, but not the other way round." He rose and went over to his bookcase, running his finger along the spines until he found the volume he wanted. "Debrett's," he said. He sat with it on his lap and leafed through it. "Here we go: Sir John Brigstock, of Hans Place in London. Widower, two sons – born in 1797 and 1799 – and one daughter. That's Sophia – a friend of Lily's. It was she who first told me of the death."

I nodded: Conant's daughter often gave her father valuable insights into the worlds of fashion and society. Having inherited her mother's beauty and ease with people and her father's intelligence and sense of humour, Lily Conant would be a match for any man – but her devotion to her father and her unwillingness to put up with any form of foppery or buffoonery meant that she would be a hard prize to win.

"Admitted a Knight Companion of the Order of the Bath in 1814, having twice been mentioned in despatches in the War of 1812," continued the magistrate.

"But you have had no word from the family about the death?" I asked.

Conant shook his head. "And nor am I likely to. Sophia sent a note to Lily yesterday talking about the 'tragic accident', but observing that her brother had always been a wild horseman. It was only the man Parker's request to see me that made me think otherwise."

"So officially..." I began.

"Officially, Sam, there is nothing to be done. But to satisfy my own curiosity I would prefer to know whether Edward Brigstock is capable of killing his own brother and, if so, why he would do it."

Something in the magistrate's tone made me pause. There were dozens, if not hundreds, of young men killed in London each year through reckless riding, so why should this instance concern him?

"Forgive me, sir, but is there anything more I should know about Mr Brigstock? Has your daughter told you much of his character?"

Conant thrust himself up out of his chair and strode over to the window. He looked out for a few moments before turning to me.

"Lily has a very dear friend, Isabel Sheridan – although we have always called her Izzy. They have been friends from childhood, and Lily mentioned a few nights ago that Izzy was being shown some preference by a young man of their acquaintance – Mr Edward Brigstock. Lily gave me to understand that things had progressed to such a stage that Izzy was expecting Brigstock to call on her papa."

"Ah," I said.

"Of course, Izzy has her own papa to protect her, but he is not privy to what we know about Edward Brigstock. The visit could still happen, of course, once Brigstock is out of mourning. And should it happen, Sam, I must know what manner of man he is. We must not deliver Izzy into the hands of a man capable of murder."

"So you see, Alice, the heavy responsibilities of being a parent," said Martha as she folded linen that evening. "One day you will have to decide whether some fellow is good enough to wed your little Martha." Alice gazed down at the tiny one asleep in her arms and bent to kiss the top of the baby's head. Our visitor was still reluctant to speak in front of me but at least now she stayed in the kitchen when I came home, rather than scuttling away into the other room, and listened with Martha to my news of the day.

I had told them of Mr Conant's concerns, leaving out some of the more disturbing details of the death of Francis Brigstock, as I needed to decide how to proceed. I could not approach Edward Brigstock himself, of course, or indeed anyone in the family, without betraying our suspicions.

"It seems to me," said Martha, patting the top of the pile of linen and turning her attention to the stove, "that the young groom might be of most help."

"Not a housemaid?" I asked. I had been thinking of using one of my favourite tricks: asking young Wilson to sweet-talk a girl into sharing information.

"What would a housemaid know about the comings and goings of the men in the family? No, you need one of the menservants – and the grooms will know when Mr Brigstock leaves the house, and perhaps even where he goes. If you follow him, you will soon build up an understanding of the man."

Alice's eyes grew rounder by the minute.

Martha was right, of course, and I decided that the next morning I would send word to Croft. Wilson had some experience of shadowing people but he needed more, and Edward Brigstock would be good practice for him.

Martha bumped me with her hip to get my attention. "You need a wash before we eat."

As I stood in the yard rinsing my hands, I heard the two women in the kitchen start to talk. Alice's voice was barely a whisper, so I had to guess what she was saying from Martha's clearer responses.

"Oh yes, Lily Conant is a very pretty girl, but not one of these silly ones who care only about the latest fashions from France. She listens as well as talking, just like you – that's a clever thing to do, because that's how you learn. If your head is always filled with the sound of your own voice, there's no room for anything else."

Alice asked something else that I couldn't catch, and Martha laughed.

"Not dozens, no, but enough. A girl like that will attract plenty of men, but some are put off when they find that she has opinions of her own, and a determination to voice them. And the ones that are scared off, well, they weren't worthy of her."

There was another muffled question from Alice.

"Now you're asking – it was a long time ago, mind you, so I'm having to think back. Three, I think – no, four. But only one that really mattered, and I accepted that one quick smart. When the right man asks you to marry him, you'll know. He may not be the richest or the handsomest, but you'll know: something in him will call to something in you."

I smiled to myself as I dried my arms and slipped back into my shirt. Martha had always insisted that mine was the first proposal she had ever received, but I had never quite believed her; she was a fine-looking girl, with a ready laugh and a sharp mind, and I can't have been the first man to notice that wonderful combination. No doubt she wanted to make me feel that my proposal had been unique, but all that mattered to me was that those three other fellows had been sent packing while I had been allowed to take her into my arms and call her mine. And I thank the heavens daily for whatever it was that she saw in me all those years ago, to make her take such a chance on me.

CHAPTER FIVE

Serle's

WEDNESDAY 26TH APRIL 1826

Wilson turned up the collar of his coat and sighed as we walked down the steps into Great Marlborough Street.

"It may not be comfortable," I said as we skirted a large puddle, "but a rainy day is perfect for what we're doing. Following someone on a bright summer's day is the Devil's own job. They loiter and gaze around them, enjoying the warmth and the sunshine and smiling at their fellow man – but on a day like today, they're so intent on getting to their destination as quickly as possible, head down against the rain, that you could follow them on an elephant and they wouldn't notice." Wilson smiled despite himself. "Well, perhaps not an elephant. But at least it's not cold. And anyway, the timing is not our choice: we must go when summoned."

That morning I had sent a message to Croft, the Brigstock groom, telling him to let us know should Edward Brigstock ask for his horse to be readied. A reply had come almost within the hour that the man would be riding out after lunch, and so we needed to be in place. We hurried along Conduit Street and Bruton Street, and took a shortcut through the formal gardens of Berkeley Square, scattering damp and disconsolate pigeons before us. We followed our noses through the grand streets of Mayfair and after about twenty minutes we emerged onto Park Lane. Hyde Park opened out before us, but we kept outside it to the east and walked on to Hyde Park Corner. The dismal weather was keeping all but the most determined sellers off the streets, and the pavement alongside the wide thoroughfare outside the marvellous Apsley House was almost deserted.

Wilson stopped to brush the rain from his shoulders, and looked down at me in almost comical misery. "Just how far is this blasted Hans Place?" he asked, wiping drops of water from the end of his nose with the back of his hand. "We'd have kept drier swimming there along the Serpentine."

"Not far now – just around the corner. We'll be in a dry cab soon enough, when we need to be." I set off again and he followed, with rather ill grace. We turned into Sloane Street, where tall brown terraces of elegant houses swept down either side, each with a short flight of steps up to a gleaming front door, and tidy railings around a small front yard. Even in the rain they looked sleek and prosperous, reminding all passers-by that here was comfortable money. Just as I felt Wilson about to protest again, I steered him into Hans Street and out into Hans Place. Its octagonal shape is rather unusual and I pointed this out to Wilson, but he simply grunted and hunched his shoulders. I sometimes forget that he is still young; children are born thinking that they are the centre of everything, and it takes many years for them to learn to look outwards and eventually realise that the world beyond themselves is so much more interesting.

"What number for the Brigstocks?" I asked as we looked around us.

"Thirty-three," said Wilson, "over there." He jerked with his head, and we walked towards the house. Two entire storeys taller than the houses in Sloane Street, these were grand properties indeed. We drew level with number thirty-three, and as Wilson slowed I chivvied him.

"Don't look at the house. Don't slow down," I advised. "Maintain the same pace, as though we have no particular interest in any one house over the others." I took my own advice, and gazed deliberately in the other direction. Thankfully the rain was easing. "Anyway, we'll not find

Croft out here – we need to report to the coach-house round the back."

We reached the end of the terrace and turned into the passageway between it and the next set of houses, and from there into the mews behind number thirty-three and its neighbours. Not many servants were around, thanks to the rain, but a scullery-maid emptying a bucket pointed us to the Brigstock premises, staring wide-eyed at Wilson. Women do seem to appreciate a tall, sturdy frame, whatever Martha may say on the matter.

No doubt waiting for us, Croft the groom was in the yard of the coach-house. He quickly ushered us out of the yard and back along the mews, checking over his shoulder all the while.

"Mr Edward is joining his sister for luncheon, but has said that he will ride out at two. I am preparing his horse now. How will you keep up with him?"

"If you can direct Wilson here to the nearest rank, he will wait around the corner in a cab."

And so it was that Wilson and I found ourselves ambling along in a cab, the jarvey under careful instructions to keep his distance from our quarry. If either of us had an-ticipated a breakneck chase through the park, we were disappointed: I doubt that a funeral procession had ever moved at a more stately pace. It was clear that, whatever his destination, Edward Brigstock was reluctant to reach it.

After nearly an hour Brigstock finally dismounted and tied his horse to the railings outside a coffeehouse. We were in Blackfriars, not far north of Waterloo Bridge and within sight of the tiered steeple of St Clement Danes. Wilson and I climbed down from the cab and I walked round to pay the jarvey.

"Your man's a lawyer, then," he said as he carefully counted out change into my palm.

"A lawyer?" I asked. "Why do you say that?"

"Serle's." He jerked his chin towards the coffeehouse. "Popular with young barristers intent on making their name. Fond of the sound of their own voices, that lot." I could well imagine. He clicked his tongue at the horses and moved off, and Wilson and I paused outside the coffeehouse. The entrance was flanked by two massive doorposts in a classical design, and even as we made to enter a group of three young men came barrelling round the corner of Portugal Street and pushed past us into Serle's.

"After you, gentlemen," said Wilson, and caught the closing door to hold it for me.

Given the hour – too late for lunch, too early for supper – Serle's was still remarkably busy, but I supposed that lawyers would call in for refreshment on their way to and from court at all hours. The wood-panelled room was divided by high-backed benches into booths, with room for up to six men in each, while cutlery, salt cellars and the like were kept on a table in the middle. Portraits of various severe-looking fellows – distinguished lawyers, at a guess – looked down over the crowd, and a large clock on one wall reminded us all of pressing engagements elsewhere.

Wilson touched my elbow and indicated the booth furthest from the entrance, where Edward Brigstock was now sitting with a tankard in front of him. One of the three men who had arrived just before us went up to him, I assume to ask if they could share his table, and Brigstock waved him away, looking past him towards the door. Wilson and I slid into a booth whose only occupant was a dusty-looking fellow of advanced years who barely glanced up from his newspaper but acknowledged our arrival with a grunt. A pot boy came over and we ordered two ales.

When our tankards arrived, Wilson lifted his with alacrity but I shook my head. He paused.

"We don't know how long we'll be waiting here," I said quietly, trying not to draw the interest of our companion. "If you drink at that rate and we're here for a couple of hours, it'll be me looking out for whoever, and you under the table."

"Aye, I can see the sense in that," said Wilson, and took the smallest bird-like sip of ale. I rolled my eyes and he smiled. Just then, a slight man with pale eyes and reddish hair came into the coffeehouse and looked around before spotting Brigstock, walking over to him and slipping into the booth opposite him. As they talked, Brigstock's face darkened. I kicked Wilson lightly under the table and indicated silently that he should try to walk past the booth to hear the gist of what was being said. But before Wilson could get to his feet, Brigstock stood abruptly.

"You'll come to regret that, sir," he said to his companion, the menace apparent in his tone. He drained his tankard, slammed it onto the table and left the coffeehouse. The man left behind sat for a moment, thoughtfully tugging on his earlobe, before walking out past us. He did not look menaced or even slightly perturbed by his encounter. As I put it to Mr Conant when I saw him that evening to add to his store of information on Edward Brigstock, I had a feeling that our gentleman was meddling in affairs of which he had little experience.

CHAPTER SIX

Comings and goings

FRIDAY 28TH APRIL 1826

Before I could act against Mrs Marwood, I needed to know more about her business. A daily report on who had attended the address would be a good start and – with Martha's pushing, as she has a soft spot for Wilson and often pleads his case with me – I had decided to allow him to take responsibility for tracking the comings and goings at the lodging house in Harrison Street. I left it to Wilson to arrange how to acquire this information, and a week after my first visit to the lodging house I was waiting in the back office of Great Marlborough Street for him to make his daily report to me.

The door to the office was nudged open and Tom Neale looked in at me.

"Waiting for young William, are you, Sam?" he asked.

I glanced up at the clock on the wall and took out my pocket watch to compare the two.

Tom came into the room and sat down. "Good lad, that one," he said conversationally. "Can think his way round a problem." He looked at me with a half-smile. "D'you know how he's managing to keep watch day and night on that lodging house of yours?" I shook my head. "He's using the message lads and their pals, working in pairs. Two of them watch the place, and every few hours one of them runs off and reports to Wilson, or to me. Some of the visitors they know by sight – you know how these message lads soon get to know anyone who might want an errand run – and the others, for a penny or two the maid will supply a name. Wilson makes sure to walk past the place himself, unannounced, two or three times a day to check that there's always someone there, watching."

"And how's he paying them?" I asked, intrigued. On only a new constable's salary and with having to give money to his mother each week, Wilson would not have much to spare.

Tom smiled wolfishly. "Have you met Wilson's sister Sally?" I shook my head. The office-keeper whistled in appreciation. "She's a beauty – even a grizzled old man like me can see it. And as for those message lads, well, they think she's the loveliest thing in London. Miss Wilson came to meet her brother here one day, and word soon went around the pack. So William offers them something better than money: each lad who helps him is invited home for tea, to gaze upon the divine Sally."

Just then the door opened and in came Wilson. Tom stood and offered him his seat.

"All well with you and the family, Mr Wilson?" he asked, winking at me.

Wilson looked from one to the other of us in confusion. "All very well, thank you, Mr Neale," he replied.

"I'm glad to hear it – it wouldn't do for Miss Wilson to be indisposed, not in the middle of this delicate operation, now, would it?" And with that the office-keeper closed the door behind him.

Wilson looked stricken. "Did he tell you?"

I held up my hand to stop him. "How you do what I ask you to do is your business, my lad. And it is a poor constable who does not learn early on that there are some things that a man craves more than money. Although I must say I am surprised that your sister agreed to your plan." The flush that spread up Wilson's neck and cheeks gave him away. "Ah. So just what have you told her about the parade of boys that you bring home with you?"

"I only take them one at a time," he explained. "And Sal thinks it's something I'm doing to help a charitable cause – showing them life as a constable, in the hope that some of them will sign up."

I laughed. "A master-stroke! Women can never resist a male who is trying to improve himself, whatever his age."

Wilson nodded eagerly. "You should see Sal talking to them and encouraging them. She's so friendly and welcoming, I've got lads queuing down the street to join the roster."

I shook my head. "She'll find out in the end, you know – they always do. But while the going's good, what do you have for me today?"

Wilson's face clouded. He took his notebook from his pocket and I held out my hand for it, but he hesitated. He looked up at me and then down at the notebook and bit his lip. Suddenly I knew.

"There's someone I know on today's list, isn't there?" I asked. "Wilson?"

He nodded and wordlessly passed me the notebook. I turned to the last few pages, found the most recent entries and read them quickly. There were three names I did not know, but among them was one I did. I looked up at Wilson.

"Are you sure it was him?"

Wilson nodded. "By coincidence, Jacob Fuller – the lad who saw him – knows him personally. He's run errands for him before – remembers him particularly for being generous and kindly." He looked down at his feet.

"I'm sorry, sir. I know he's a friend of yours. I was in two minds..."

I held up my hand to silence him. "We must focus on the deed and not the doer. The deed remains the same." But I will confess that I was horrified.

CHAPTER SEVEN

Bruises and confessions

MONDAY 1ST MAY 1826

A few days later, my suspicion about Brigstock being out of his depth was proved right. That morning I was waiting in the front office, leaning against the desk and looking at the three rogues lined up on the bench.

"On your feet, lads – you're up next." Albert Wayman, one of my fellow constables, rolled his eyes at me as he pushed his charges towards the door of the courtroom.

"Busy morning, Bert?" I asked.

"Three warrants from Mr Conant, disorderly conduct, and I found the three of them supping together. My lucky day, you might say – their love of the ale saved me a deal of walking. All going before Mr Dawson."

And with that, Bert and the three scoundrels disappeared into the courtroom. I went through to the back office, and to my surprise Bert joined me there only ten minutes later.

"More of Mr Dawson's special verdicts," he said conversationally. "Nice and quick, they are."

I looked up from my notebook. "Special verdicts?" I asked.

"My three disorderlies," he said. "Straightforward as you like, known for it, found ape-drunk – and acquitted." He winked at me. "Not all magistrates are as dedicated as Mr Conant. Mr Dawson, now, he likes to clear the court as quickly as he can."

And as if on cue, the door opened and Tom Neale looked round it.

"You're wanted, Sam," he said. "Courtroom – Mr Dawson. He's not happy, so you'd better hurry."

"You are not John Conant's private constable, Plank – you would do well to remember that. As would he."

The court clerk looked studiously at his papers as Mr Dawson thundered at me. It seemed that the magistrate was using the time he had saved by acquitting Bert's three prisoners to give me a dressing down. He glowered at me from the bench, where his considerable girth filled the chair and his jowls shook with outrage.

"Several times this month I have called for a constable to execute my warrants, and have been sent more junior men. Just occasionally I expect to be offered your services, sir, as our most experienced constable, but time and again I am told that you are conducting enquiries for Conant. And when I ask him just what enquiries are so important, he fobs me off with some story or other."

I kept my head bowed. Here we were approaching the truth of the matter – that Mr Dawson felt excluded by Mr Conant – but he could not show his anger to his equal and, like all bullies, turned his ire instead on those under his control. As a younger man I would have bucked against him, determined to win the argument at any cost, but years of dealing with such men have taught me that the most sensible approach is this: silence, contrition, and then business as usual.

"D'you hear me, sir?" Dawson barked. The clerk shuffled some more papers.

I looked up at the bench, my hands clasped behind me. "I do, sir. And if I have given the appearance of favouring the work of one magistrate over another, I must apologise." The clerk looked at me sharply; his years of experience had taught him to recognise a carefully-worded sentence when he heard one. I ignored him and continued. "If you have any warrants today that require immediate attention, I am at your service."

"Two – one affray, one burglary." The magistrate gestured to the clerk, who held up the warrants. I stepped over to his desk and took them.

"I shall see to these immediately, your worship," I said. "Immediately." And I bowed slightly for more emphasis.

"Hmmm," grunted Dawson, and waved his hand to signal that I was dismissed.

I returned to the back office and was just sitting down to read the first of the warrants when Tom put his head round the door.

"You'd better come quickly, Sam – there's a young groom asking for you. Croft, he said his name was."

Out by Tom's counter, the Brigstock groom Croft was bending over holding his sides – he had obviously been running and was still catching his breath. Tom came up behind me, took a look at the lad, and said, "Tea, I think." Our office keeper was always good at knowing when to make himself scarce.

I took hold of Croft's arm and steered him to the bench, sitting down beside him. He panted a few more times and then turned to look at me.

"It's Mr Edward, sir. He's been hurt. Not far from here, and I thought you..." he tailed off. Tom came back into the room just in time to see me leaving with Croft. Wilson was walking up the steps into the office as we opened the door, so I told him to turn round and come

with us. He glanced at the warrants in my hand, and I
ducked back in to give the papers to Tom.

"I suppose I'll have to explain to Mr Dawson that
you've been called out unexpectedly," he said.

"He might be happier if you just said that I had
dropped dead."

"He might indeed. I'll consider it."

Wilson and I followed Croft at a smart pace out along
Great Marlborough Street, into Carnaby Street and then
into Tyler Court. Just before the new Craven Chapel,
with its austere Roman frontage, the groom turned into
an alleyway. Down at the end of it I could see two horses,
and a shape on the ground – Edward Brigstock.

Croft bent down to him and shook him by the shoulder. "Sir, sir – it's me, Croft. I've brought help."

Brigstock groaned, and as he turned his face to me I
could see that he had taken something of a beating. One
eye was already swollen closed, and there was a nasty gash
alongside the other one. His top lip was split, and from
the way he held his right arm with the left it was clear that
something had gone wrong with his shoulder.

"Can you stand, sir?" I asked.

He mumbled something and held out his good arm.
Wilson took hold of the wrist and the elbow and with
great gentleness levered Brigstock to his feet.

"I think he'll do best on his horse," suggested Wilson, and when I nodded he made a stirrup of his hands for Brigstock. With Croft pushing up from below, they managed to get him seated. Croft untied both animals and we headed back to Great Marlborough Street, with Wilson going on ahead to warn Mr Conant and suggest that a surgeon be called.

If Mr Conant was surprised to have a battered and bleeding man carried up to his dining room and settled into his armchair, he hid it admirably. Doctor Weston arrived quickly, inspected the patient and declared him likely to live, albeit badly bruised for a few days and with a broken collarbone. He turned up his cuffs and sponged off the worst of the blood before tying a triangular cloth into a sling and carefully manoeuvring Brigstock's right arm into it.

"No riding for six weeks, no lemonade until that lip heals, and no fisticuffs for as long as you can manage it," he said gruffly before leaving.

Conant waited until the surgeon had gone before picking up one of the dining chairs and placing it carefully in front of the armchair. He indicated to me that Croft, Wilson and I should likewise seat ourselves, behind him but so that Edward Brigstock could see all of us. When we were all in place, the magistrate began.

"Well now, sir," he said, "I think we need to talk about what has happened to you." Brigstock looked at him with his one good eye but said nothing. "And don't even consider telling me that you fell off your horse." Still nothing. "In that case, perhaps we should begin with Mr Croft." Conant turned his chair so that he could see the groom.

Croft looked very uncomfortable and glanced at Brigstock, but said nothing.

"Your loyalty to your master does you credit, my boy," said Conant, "but if we are to apprehend those responsible, you must both tell the truth. You first, and then Mr Brigstock."

The groom twisted his hands together and looked again at Brigstock, who shrugged. "Go ahead, Croft," he said thickly, putting a finger to his wounded lip as he tried to talk. "Tell them what you know."

Croft swallowed hard and then started to speak. "When Mr Francis was alive, he came to this part of town quite regularly. About once a fortnight. Sometimes I rode with him part of the way, sometimes he mentioned afterwards where he'd been, when I said that his horse was tired." He paused. "He never said what he was doing here, but I assumed he was visiting a lady."

Conant nodded. "A fair assumption."

"And then after he died, Mr Edward started doing the same. Only more often – once a week now, for the past month."

Brigstock grunted. "How do you know so much?"

"Your horse comes back tired, just like Mr Francis's did. And I have friends who see you – jarveys, and other grooms. That perfect star on Beacon's face is easy to recognise."

I had noticed it myself; Brigstock's horse was a fine-looking animal.

"Please continue, Croft," said Conant. "What happened today?"

"When Mr Edward came to the yard this morning, he seemed very agitated – even Beacon noticed it. Do you remember, sir, how hard he was to mount?" Croft looked at Brigstock, who nodded reluctantly. "And so I decided that I would follow him." He leaned forward in his chair. "I'm sorry, sir, I know I did wrong, but after losing Mr Francis like that, and with you seeming so upset – I though Beacon might bolt or throw you. I saddled up Marjorie and followed you."

"And Mr Brigstock led you to an alley off Carnaby Street?" asked the magistrate.

Croft shook his head. "No: first he went into a coffee-house on Broad Street. He was in there for about ten minutes, then came out with three men and they forced him along Marshall Street. I had to untie both horses and follow a way behind to keep out of sight, and by the time I found Mr Edward, he was in that alleyway and the three men had gone."

"Thank you, Mr Croft – very clear." Conant turned his chair again so that he was looking directly at Brigstock. "So, Mr Brigstock – we now know when and how you ended up being beaten to within an inch of your life in a Piccadilly alleyway. What we do not yet know is why. And you are going to tell us." He paused. "Unless you want me to send word to your father, and he can come and ask you the same question."

Brigstock shook his head and winced. "No need for that," he said, "but Croft, you can go."

The groom stood.

"Take him down to the front office if you would, Constable Wilson," said Conant. "Ask the office keeper for a hot drink, and Constable Plank will be down to see you soon."

The door closed behind Croft and Wilson. Brigstock grunted quietly as he adjusted his position in the chair and then he started talking, looking directly at neither of us but rather past us into the distance, licking his swollen lips between sentences.

"Francis was always a fool. I know older brothers often think that of younger ones, but he genuinely was. He squandered every opportunity our father offered him, every chance he had at making something of himself. If there was trouble within ten miles, Francis was drawn to it as to a magnet." He shook his head sadly. "About two years ago he started coming into town regularly, just as Croft said. Twice a month, sometimes more. At first I assumed he had a woman somewhere. But then there was the money. He spent more and more, borrowing from me and from friends, and even taking trinkets from the house to sell. A woman can be expensive, to be sure, but this was something else. I could tell from his desperation. A woman – even a demanding one – should make you happy, not miserable." He tried to smile, but it ended in a grimace as his bruises made themselves felt.

"And so last month I resolved to have it out with him. I invited him to go riding with me, just we two. I told him what I had noticed of his behaviour. He blustered for a while, but at last he admitted what was happening." Edward Brigstock looked down at his hands and shook his head disbelievingly. "He was being blackmailed. Someone had found out where he was going all those times, and was threatening to denounce him to the courts." He looked up at us, pain clear in his eyes. "To the courts. To denounce him as a sodomite."

"Ah," said Conant. "I see."

Brigstock leaned forward. "But you don't see – not at all. The threat was effective, to be sure, but it was a lie. My brother was not a sodomite. Far from it. His tastes lay entirely elsewhere." He stopped and looked beseechingly at the magistrate. "Francis liked girls, Mr Conant.

Young girls. Unspoilt girls. And he found someone who could offer him a steady supply."

The bile rose in my throat as a vision of the oleaginous Mother Marwood came to me. Perhaps she had been his source.

"Of course such a preference, if known, could damage his marriage prospects," Brigstock went on. "Not that Francis was keen to marry, given his tastes, but my parents had it in mind for him. And so my idiot brother paid his tormenters for their silence." Brigstock slumped back in his chair. "I was furious when he told me – disgusted to hear of his dalliances, angry that he had dragged our name into such filth. We argued and I lashed out with my crop. I missed him, but caught his mount." Brigstock's voice caught. "The animal bolted and Francis was unseated. He fell awkwardly, hitting his head. I leapt off Beacon and ran over to him. I put my hand behind his head to help him sit, and – and there was blood. Too much blood. He looked up at me, tried to speak, and died in my arms." Brigstock let his head fall back against the chair and closed his eyes. "God forgive me," he said quietly, "but I was relieved. It meant that I wouldn't have to tell my father – my sister! – what Francis had done."

The relief of confession was plain to see on the man's face. With the skill of the best of his profession, Conant pressed on while the man was in the mood for disclosure.

"And what has brought you to this sorry state today?"

Brigstock smiled ruefully, wincing as his torn lip pulled. "You gentlemen will doubtless think me naïve, but I believed that with my brother's death the demands for money would cease. But they did not; if anything, they became more urgent, more greedy. I received a message saying that if I did not hand over payments when and where instructed, the truth about Francis's visits would be made public. I did not dare take a chance; Miss Harriette Wilson has taught us that lesson."

We could all remember the outcry and embarrassment that had ensued when the commercially-minded courtesan had published her memoirs some months before, naming many of her lovers.

"That explains your meeting with the well-dressed young fellow in Serle's last Wednesday," I suggested. Brigstock looked at me sharply, then nodded.

"And much good it did me. I considered going to my father," he continued, "telling him that Francis had accumulated gambling debts and asking for money to settle them, but I feared it would lead only to more questions. And so I tried to keep the payments going myself."

Conant shook his head sadly. "The blackmailer is a strange beast, is he not, constable?"

I nodded – I have met many in my time. "The strangeness of the beast, sir," I said to Brigstock, "is that feeding him simply makes him hungrier. His is an appetite that can never be sated."

"And so I have found," he agreed. "Today I had to tell them that I have no money left to pay. They told me to go to my father, and I refused. And you can see their response to that." He indicated his damaged face.

Just then the clock struck the hour. Conant glanced up at it and then back at Brigstock. The poor man looked exhausted. The magistrate stood and put his chair back near the table.

"You will spend the night here, Edward – it would be a cruelty to send you home to your sister in that state. Croft can settle your horse in my stable and then return to Hans Place to tell your father that you are staying with a friend. And tomorrow, you and I will sit down with Constable Plank and see what plan we can formulate."

"Blackmail is a serious crime, is it not?" asked Martha, her back to me as she scraped the plates after dinner. Alice had taken little Martha out for a walk; it had become her habit of an evening, and Martha encouraged anything that gave the new mother more confidence.

"Extremely serious," I agreed. "Transportation for life in some cases."

"And why is it so harshly punished?"

I thought for a moment. "I suppose it is because black-mail threatens to take from a man his most prized posses-sion – his good reputation. And once lost, it is all but impossible to regain."

Martha turned and leaned against the cupboard, her arms folded. "But surely, if the man is guilty of what they say he has done – or worse – then he deserves what is said about him. Indeed, perhaps it should be made public what he is doing."

"You mean Francis Brigstock," I said. Martha nodded. "But if that were the test, then we should always have to find out first whether what is said is the truth. And don't forget that we have found out about this blackmail by ac-cident – Francis Brigstock did not report it. So perhaps that is what happens: those who are guilty of what they are accused of doing will pay up in silence, while those who are innocent of it will come to us."

"But why waste time on Brigstock? You know that he did those things – his brother told you as much."

"And Edward Brigstock is now paying the price – lit-erally – for his brother's actions. You see, blackmail is greedy: allowed to flourish, it will consume all in its path."

CHAPTER EIGHT

Setting the trap

TUESDAY 2ND MAY 1826

The next morning Martha was quiet as she prepared breakfast. I had sensed her awake beside me once or twice in the night, looking up at the ceiling as she thought things through, and so I was not surprised when she sat down beside me after we had eaten and asked me to listen.

"I have been thinking about Edward Brigstock," she said. "I have no doubt that you and William could soon run his blackmailers to ground: that one you saw in Serle's wasn't smart enough to realise that he was being watched, and your message lads will be able to tell you who forced Mr Brigstock out of the coffeehouse in Broad Street – there's little that escapes their notice." I nodded in agreement. "But that will solve only one part of the problem."

I smiled at her. "Are you telling me, Mrs Plank, that years of being married to a constable and listening to him talk about his work have made you cynical?"

"Well, if you insist on talking so much, what choice do I have but to listen?" she said archly. "My concern about Edward Brigstock is that if you choke off the blackmailers, they will take fright and you will lose your chance to follow them further up the chain."

"You talk now of a chain of criminals, then?"

"Don't tease me, Sam – not if you value coming home to a good supper and a warm bed." I held up my hands in surrender. "All I am saying is that you could turn these blackmailers to your advantage – let them give you something rather than taking all the time."

But although I was teasing her, I had to admit that she had raised an important consideration: was the man in Serle's the upright man, or just a rogue?

I always think well while walking, and by the time I arrived at Great Marlborough Street I had devised a trap. I asked to see Mr Conant and his overnight guest and described it to them. The magistrate said nothing; he simply stood with his back to the window. To his credit, Edward Brigstock did not dismiss my plan out of hand; he listened in silence, with only the occasional raised eyebrow betraying any reaction.

"And so you see, Mr Brigstock, we would very much need you," I said in conclusion. "There would be danger, of course. We would do our utmost to minimise it by accompanying you at a distance," I looked over at Conant and he nodded, "but there would be danger. That said, the scheme could not work without you."

I waited. Some men need cajoling and enticing, but I sensed that Brigstock was one who would back away if he felt that he was being led unwillingly. With such men, it is best to leave them with the facts and allow them time to reach their own decision. The magistrate obviously felt the same way; he did not add anything, but idly scratched his chin and looked out of the window.

"Would I need to give real information, do you think?" asked Brigstock after a couple of minutes.

I leaned forward. "If we get our timing right, sir," I said, "you will not have to give any specific information, real or false. The aim is only to convince them that you have such information – not to hand it over."

"And you – both of you – think that this is our best chance of uncovering whoever made my brother's life so miserable?"

Conant looked earnestly at Brigstock and spoke with conviction. "There are no guarantees, Edward – we are dealing with ruthless and unpredictable men who are willing to ruin other people for personal profit. But they are driven by their desire for money, and this will not be the first time that Constable Plank has come up against such people."

Time was of the essence: we needed Edward Brigstock to confront his tormenter while he was still angry about his beating and determined to put an end to the blackmail. And eventually Brigstock agreed to send a message via one of our lads to the only name he had been given – a Mr Smith, to be reached at Serle's. I doubted that was his real name, but no matter.

A reply came quickly: Brigstock was to go to the coffeehouse on Friday morning at eleven, with his next payment.

CHAPTER NINE

Charitable intentions

WEDNESDAY 3RD MAY 1826

Although I had delayed several days since Wilson's shocking revelation, I could put this visit off no longer. As I stood outside the narrow building near the corner of Cheapside and Milk Street, it came to me that it was almost exactly a year since I had first called at these premises. The man I had come to see had been a stranger to me then, but over the past year I had grown to know, trust and indeed admire him, which made my task this day all the more unpleasant. But, as I had advised Wilson when he had shown me that list of visitors to the lodging house in Harrison Street, my job was to focus on the deed, and the vileness of that deed had to trump any gentler feelings of friendship or sentimentality.

I pushed open the heavy door and walked into the small banking hall; apart from one gentleman talking to the chief clerk, I was the only visitor. Stevenson, the junior clerk, looked up from his ledger and smiled at me in recognition. He glanced across at Mr Harris, and the chief clerk jerked his head towards the back rooms of the bank.

Stevenson hopped down off his stool and came over to me, taking my hat from me. "If you'd care to follow me, sir, Mr Freame is in the parlour."

"My dear Plank!" Edward Freame rose from his chair with a wide smile and took my outstretched hand in both of his. The newspaper he had been reading fell to the floor, and Stevenson picked it up, folded it and placed it on the table. "Tea, I think, Stevenson, if you'd be so kind. And perhaps given the hour," he glanced at the clock on the mantelpiece, "we might venture a small piece of that delicious gingerbread that your mother so thoughtfully sent in with you today." The young clerk blushed with pleasure and left the parlour.

The banker settled back into his own armchair and indicated that I should take the other. He smiled broadly again, and then looked at me more enquiringly as he realised that I was not returning his smile with quite as much vigour.

"Ah: I see from your face that you are calling on me today as a constable rather than as a friend," he said. "Nevertheless, I shall do all I can to help." He folded his hands neatly in his lap and waited a minute or two. "A matter of some delicacy, then." I nodded. "Out with it, Sam – out with it."

I took a deep breath. "Recently I, well, we – Martha and I, that is – we took in a young woman and her new-born baby." I paused. Freame waited in silence. "It became clear to us that she was a very young woman – a girl, to be honest, aged only fourteen." The banker tutted sympathetically but said nothing. "My wife gained her confidence, and it seems that this girl has been working as a prostitute." I searched Freame's face for shock or disgust – or guilt – but found nothing. "She boards at a lodging-house, and the landlady is involved in the trade – in supplying young girls to men whose tastes run to the juvenile." I finished in a rush.

Just then the door opened and Stevenson came in, bearing a tea-tray. He put it on the table and carefully laid out the cups and plates before withdrawing. Freame leaned forward to pour the tea and handed me a cup before sitting back to sip his own.

"Do you wish me to recommend this young girl for a position?" he asked. "With a young baby it is a little more difficult, but I know some good Quaker families who might take her in and..." He stopped when he saw me shaking my head.

I put down my cup. "My interest is more general. I am keen to put this lodging-house and its repugnant landlady out of business. I want to find the men who, who," I waved my hand to save having to say the words, "and warn them off. To this end, I have had the premises watched, and a note taken of all visitors. And the note of Friday's visitors included you."

Freame blinked at me. "Me? Visiting a brothel?" He frowned in recollection. "Friday, you say." He reached into his pocket and took out a small appointments book. Turning to the relevant page, he ran his finger down it. "But the only call I made on Friday was to Mrs Marwood's premises in Bloomsbury – Harrison Street. One of our charitable enterprises: a home for orphaned girls." He stopped and looked up at me with horror on his face.

I shook my head sadly. "Mrs Marwood is no kindly soul. I fear that you and your fellow benefactors have been misled as to the true nature of her interest in those girls."

"That poor man," said Martha with feeling as I recounted our meeting to her that evening. "How long has he been giving money to this Marwood creature?"

"It was not so much money as general assistance. The property in Harrison Street is owned by a group of successful Quaker men of business. Good souls, all of them, committed to making life better for their fellow men."

"I know how admiring you are of Mr Freame," said Martha, "but how did he become muddled up with Mother Marwood?"

"About six years ago the Quakers' meeting house in Gracechurch Street burnt down. While they were raising funds to rebuild it, Mr Freame told me, he and many others would meet instead a couple of miles north in Stoke Newington. A project that they had had in mind for some time was a school for girls," my wife nodded approvingly at this, "and when a property in Stoke Newington became available, they decided to go ahead. Fleetwood House, it's called. They teach all manner of interesting things – astronomy, physics, Latin, German – and there is plenty of land for the girls to run around. They even have their own transport: to get to their rebuilt meeting house in Gracechurch Street, the young ladies from the school are taken in a carriage with bench seats – twenty-five at a time!"

"What a lark that must be," said my wife, shaking her head in wonder. "How I should have loved to go to school, Sam – and how pleased I am to know that other girls are being given that chance." She sat silently for a few moments, gazing into the distance, before drawing herself back to our current problem. "But how is the Harrison Street lodging house part of the story?"

"Well," I said, leaning forward on my elbows, "the Quakers' interest in the care and education of young girls did not go unnoticed. And Mrs Marwood, scenting an opportunity, approached Mr Freame about three years ago with an idea. She said that she had long been concerned about the plight of young girls whose parents had died – boys were able to make their own way but girls, she said, were more vulnerable. As a young widow, went her story, she knew that she would never have children of her own, but felt that God had called her to look after these poor orphans. A premises on Harrison Street was for sale, she said, that would make a perfect home for her and her charges."

"But your Mr Freame is an educated man – a banker. He would not be easy to fool," said Martha with some feeling.

"He was not easy to fool, not at all," I agreed. "He told me that he checked her story carefully. A Mrs Elizabeth Marwood had been widowed in 1819, her late husband a bookbinder. When he presented the proposal to his fellow Friends, they agreed that the Society would buy the property and retain the title, and let Mrs Marwood live there as guardian for up to fourteen girls aged between eight and fifteen. A monthly stipend would be paid to Mrs Marwood to feed and clothe the girls, and they would be enrolled in the local charity school. Mr Freame was appointed overseer of the home, and as such he visits every other month – his most recent visit being last Friday."

"Did he suspect nothing?" asked Martha. "What did he see when he went?"

"His visits were never unannounced, so Mother Marwood had plenty of time to prepare. The house was always spotless, he said, with the girls sleeping two or three to a room. The kitchen was well-provisioned. Each time he called he would be presented with two girls so that he could inspect their clothing and general health – but again, Marwood would select who to show him." I paused, and my sharp-eyed wife missed nothing.

"What, Sam? Did one of the girls tell him something?"

I shook my head. "No, nothing like that; according to Mr Freame, Marwood was careful never to leave him alone with them. He thought that it was for their protection, but now he sees that it was for hers. But he did say that on the last couple of visits, he thought that the girls he met seemed uneasy – scared, even. When he questioned Marwood, she explained that the girls were recent arrivals who were recovering from earlier mistreatment."

"When in reality she was the one mistreating them." Martha reached into her apron pocket for a handkerchief and dabbed at her eyes. "And doubtless the sight of another man inspecting them filled them with terror.

Thank heavens you found Alice that night, Sam – she at least we can save."

"Indeed," I said. "I have made enquiries at the office and elsewhere, and am reasonably confident of finding her a position before too long. With little Martha, of course."

"But what of this wicked Marwood woman? What are you going to do about her?"

"As ever, my dear, we will need patience. Much as I would like to close down her racket right now, and throw her into the Thames, bag and baggage, that would not serve us well. We will continue to watch Harrison Street: we need more names and more evidence of her trade." I reached across the table and put my hand on Martha's. "I know you want to bring all of those girls back here and tuck them into bed alongside our little Alice, but you cannot. Hard though it is, we need them to remain where they are so that Marwood suspects nothing."

"Bait, you mean?" said Martha bitterly.

I squeezed the hand I was holding. "The girls under Marwood's roof have already been... damaged. There is nothing we can do to undo that, but as soon as we can we will rescue them and try to make amends. By sacrificing them – and it is a sacrifice, my dear, that sickens me as it sickens you – we may protect many more from their fate."

Martha pulled her hand away and gave me a level look. "No child should ever be a sacrifice," she said quietly.

CHAPTER TEN

The errand boy

FRIDAY 5TH MAY 1826 – MORNING

O n the Friday specified in the note we had received from Mr Smith, I spent an hour in the morning rehearsing with Edward Brigstock. I would accompany him, of course, and Wilson would come too; having seen the treatment that the blackmailers were willing to mete out to even a fit young man like Brigstock, I thought it prudent to level the odds with a strong constable. By half-past ten Wilson and I were once again in Serle's, a tankard of ale in front of each of us. I sat myself with my back to the booth where Brigstock had settled, so that I could both see Mr Smith arrive and overhear their conversation. Wilson faced me – and therefore the bench that we had left for Mr Smith – so that he could watch for any threatening behaviour.

As the bell of St Clement Danes tolled the hour, the door to the coffeehouse opened to admit our Mr Smith – it was indeed the man we had seen before with Edward Brigstock. He spotted his quarry in the booth and walked over to him, pausing to have a word with the proprietor on his way past. I heard him slide into the booth, and the proprietor came over with a glass of claret. Wilson lifted his tankard to his lips and looked past me. For my part, I leaned back and shook out the newspaper I was holding.

"Mr Brigstock," said the new arrival, "I am pleased to hear that you have had a change of heart."

"It was not my heart that concerned your crew, but rather my face."

"It is unfortunate that you were so... resistant," said Mr Smith smoothly. "But you have seen the error of your ways, which is wise." I heard him swallow his wine. "I have only a few minutes to spare, Mr Brigstock, so if you could just hand over what you owe. You can be grateful that I have not shared our little disagreement with my superiors; experience has shown me that most gentlemen come to their senses after one warning, and there is no need to blot their copybook."

So Martha's instinct had been right: Smith was acting on the orders of others. I waited, ears pricked: would Brigstock stick to our plan, or would the sight of Smith, and the none too subtle reminder of the fists for hire at Smith's command, frighten him? I heard the bench creak as Brigstock shifted in his seat, and then he spoke. "If you can spare a minute or two, Mr Smith, I would like to propose a slightly different arrangement."

I caught Wilson's eye, and he nodded very slightly; I had told him of our plan while we were walking to Serle's, and he knew what I was hoping to hear.

There was a long silence. "A different arrangement?" asked Smith eventually. "What did you have in mind, Mr Brigstock?"

"As you know from your surveillance, my family has connections," said Brigstock. "And through these connections, I frequently come to hear of, shall we say, indiscretions. My late brother's dalliances were small fry compared to these." He paused. Good: I had stressed that he needed to feign reluctance and discomfort, if Smith was to trust him.

"Go on, Mr Brigstock," said Smith. "You are among friends here."

Wilson's eyes widened, as – I am sure – did mine.

Edward Brigstock continued quietly. "If I were to hear of anything that might interest you and your superiors, might we consider such information as my payment? On a regular basis? After all, if I were to give you the wherewithal to enter into your own arrangements with others, that would surely be worth many times what I am paying you presently. The goose that lays the golden egg, as they say."

There was another creak; I guessed that Smith was leaning forward. Brigstock was reeling in our fish.

"I think I can say, Mr Brigstock, that we would be most interested in such an exchange. On a regular basis, you say. Have you anything to pass on today, then?"

I could hear the smile in Brigstock's voice; like us, he could tell that the balance of power had shifted in his favour. "There is just one more thing, Mr Smith." He dropped his voice a tone or two. "For such sensitive matters, I feel – and I hope that you will not take this amiss – that I must insist on dealing with someone more senior." I saw Wilson's eyes flicker to where Smith was sitting; he had learnt quickly that a man's reaction was shown more truthfully in his face than in his words. Brigstock continued. "I am sure you can appreciate, Mr Smith, that sharing information is an altogether more sensitive and dangerous transaction than simply handing over money. If I am to betray my friends and acquaintances – if I am to risk censure and social exile – I need to look into the eyes of the man who will be taken into my confidence. And not just those of his errand boy."

It was a risk. We had deliberated over those words. Was errand boy too harsh? Would Smith take offence and turn on his heel? But Brigstock needed to reassert his superiority, if Smith was to believe that he had the elevated contacts he claimed. I found that I was holding my breath.

Perhaps a minute passed. And then Smith spoke. "Very well, Mr Brigstock. I will take your proposal to my superiors, and we will send you word of when and where our next meeting will be." He stood, and then I heard him speak almost in my ear; I guessed he was leaning over to whisper to Brigstock as he passed. "And if it is determined that your next meeting will after all be with me, sir, you had better make sure your affairs are in order before you set out. I am nobody's errand boy."

Once he had left the coffeehouse I nodded at Wilson and he followed Smith out. Two minutes later Wilson returned. "He's gone," he confirmed. "I watched him until he turned into Chancery Lane."

In that case," I said, "you may join us, Mr Brigstock."

Edward Brigstock stood and walked round to our booth. As he leaned on the table to steady himself as he slid onto the bench, I saw that his hands were trembling.

"An excellent performance," I said approvingly. "I think you pitched it well."

"You didn't see his face," said Brigstock. Wilson slid a glass across the table to him and he took a deep drink. "I don't think I'm cut out for this at all." He drained the glass. "Do you think Smith's superiors will take up the offer?"

"Almost certainly," I said. "The one advantage of dealing with criminals who worship money above all else is that you always know how to tempt them. Smith's associates are making a bit of money from you now, but we've given them the prospect of making much more money through you in the future – and they won't be able to resist."

"Through me?" said Brigstock. "Through me? Will I have to meet them?"

I shook my head. "Forgive me: I was careless with my words. If all goes as I hope it will, that was your last encounter with Mr Smith or any of his friends. Talking of which, Wilson, could you possibly ask the proprietor to step over here."

A few minutes later a man of about my own age came over, wiping his hands on his apron. He looked tired and hot but ventured a smile.

"Good morning, gentlemen," he said, his practised eye taking in our table and its setting. "May I offer you some food – the venison is uncommonly good today."

I shifted along the bench and indicated that the proprietor should join us. He looked around the room, saw that all customers had been attended to, and took a seat with a grateful sigh.

"I am Constable Samuel Plank, of Great Marlborough Street," I said. The man's smile faded a little; I find that constables are rarely welcomed with rapture. "And your name, please, sir?"

"George Moore," he replied.

"And you are the proprietor? Responsible for these premises and all that happens on them?"

He nodded, frowning. "In partnership with Mr Harvey, yes." He looked at each of us in turn. "Is there a problem with my measures, sir? We have done our best to use the new units, but some of the older customers..." His voice trailed off as I shook my head.

"We are not here to check that you are using the imperial gallon. But I do have a concern." The look of relief that had flashed across Moore's face disappeared as I said this. "It seems that your coffeehouse is being used to perpetrate blackmail."

Moore turned pale. "Blackmail?" he repeated. "But how?" He looked wildly about him, as though expecting to see scoundrels under every table.

"Do you recognise this gentleman?" I asked him, indicating Edward Brigstock.

Moore nodded. "I have seen him in here twice now – one day last week, and then again today."

I was pleased: he obviously had an excellent memory for faces.

"You will remember, then, that on both occasions he met the same man."

Moore nodded slowly. "Is that the...?" he asked.

"He has threatened Mr Brigstock, yes. And, as I say, on your premises."

The proprietor blinked rapidly. "But you can't expect me to listen in on every conversation, to hear every word that is said. This is a coffeehouse near the Inns of Court – some of the most talkative people in the kingdom come here every day!"

"Indeed, indeed," I said. "And of course we do not expect you to eavesdrop on them. But now that we have brought this matter to your attention, as a law-abiding man of business I am sure you will want to do all that you can to ensure that no such threats are made again." Moore nodded with relief. "The man whom Mr Brigstock met called himself Mr Smith, and indeed has messages sent to him here under that name. We suspect that this is not his real name. And we would very much like to know that real name."

Moore bit on his lip as he thought, and quickly came to a decision. "Willoughby. John Willoughby."

Something about the name was familiar. Wilson looked at me; he was becoming remarkably adept at reading my face. "Sir?" he asked. "Have you had dealings with Mr Willoughby? A previous incident?"

I shook my head. It was there, but I couldn't quite grasp it. And then it came to me. I looked at Wilson. "He's a clerk at Hatton Garden."

"A lawyer's clerk?" asked Wilson.

I shook my head.   "Hatton Garden," I repeated. "Clerkenwell court."

CHAPTER ELEVEN

The duties of the office

FRIDAY 5TH MAY 1826 – AFTERNOON

T he revelation that Smith was in fact Willoughby, and a clerk at the court in Hatton Garden, troubled me greatly as it complicated our next steps in a manner that I had not foreseen. I needed to discuss my concerns with someone, and after I had sent Wilson back to his duties at Great Marlborough Street I reflected on how fortunate I was to have several people whom I could take into my confidence. There was Martha, of course, with her uncanny understanding of human nature, but it would be difficult for her to grasp the legal sensitivities of the situation. The banker Freame had often shown himself to be a talented moral arbiter – but perhaps a purely moral approach was too simplistic in this case. What I needed was someone who understood the delicacy of what I had potentially exposed, and so it was that I headed southwards, then turned left into Temple Bar and walked almost unseeing along Fleet Street. At Farringdon-circus I jostled my way across and struck for Ludgate Hill, covering my mouth against the dust from the building works for the new market. It was a journey I could have made in my sleep.

I banged on the heavy wooden door. The warder hauled it open and gave me a nod; my work took me to Newgate often enough for my face to be familiar. I stepped into the prison precincts and shivered; the atmosphere within the thick walls was chilling in both senses of the word.

"Is Mr Wontner here?" I asked.

"Aye, the keeper's at his papers," said the warder, "although I daresay he'll be glad of an excuse to do something else." He led me across the yard and into the corridor leading to John Wontner's office. "I'll leave you here sir, as you know the way. As a rule, we're more concerned with people breaking out than breaking in." And his weathered face broke into something that I supposed was a smile, before he touched his hand to his forehead and walked off.

I knocked on Wontner's door, and pushed it open as he called, "Come!"

The warder had been right; the poor man was sitting behind a veritable mound of papers, some of which had spilled off his desk and onto the floor. I went to pick them up but he put up his hands in surrender. "Don't bother, Sam – I'll almost certainly push them off again. Now please tell me that you have come on extremely urgent business that will require me to give you my full attention." He sat back in his chair with relief. "The only time I really curse the blasted animal that landed on me is when the paperwork threatens to reach higher than my own head."

John Wontner had been a marshal in the city, until one day something caused his horse to rear up and then fall on him. They saved his life but not his leg, and – looking for a job that would tolerate a peg-leg – he became keeper of Newgate. But it's an ill wind, as Martha frequently reminds me, and, with his interest in justice and his compassion for his fellow man, Wontner had done much to improve both the prison and the lot of those who found themselves within its confines. At the core of his success, I had often thought, was his ability to listen more than he talked – a quality that is rarer than it should be.

"Urgent to me, yes," I replied. "Wilson and I have come across a situation that is uncommonly delicate, not to say complicated, and I would very much value your opinion as to how I should – perhaps even could – proceed."

"Delicate and complicated, you say," said Wontner with a wink. "In that case, I shall most definitely need a clear desk." And with great satisfaction he gathered the papers into rough piles and deposited them on the floor. "With any luck, some of our resident rats will perform the first useful service of their lives and gnaw their way through that lot. Barley water?"

Wontner had once confided in me that savage beatings at the hands of a drunken father, coupled with what he saw in his prison on a daily basis, had convinced him of the merits of temperance, and anyone visiting him would be offered only tea or barley water. A large earthenware jug of the latter lived permanently in his office, and I will confess that I have grown quite fond of the taste, which I now associate with good company and sensible conversation. I took a tumbler from him, and watched as he poured his own, took a deep draught and smacked his lips before settling back in his chair in the manner of one looking forward to a good story.

I did my best. I told him about the Brigstock brothers, Francis's death, the beating suffered by Edward, my plan to ensnare the blackmailers, and finally our discovery of the real identity of Mr Smith. I tried not to embellish with opinion or supposition, but to stick to the facts. If you want a man's honest opinion about something, you cannot hobble him with your own. When I had finished speaking, I drained my tumbler and waited.

"Clerkenwell court, you say," said Wontner at last. I nodded. He reached behind him for a book and leafed through it; it was his well-thumbed copy of Kent's London directory. "Ah, here we go: police offices and magistrates. Hatton Garden... Magistrates: Harmon Percival Esquire, Allan Laing Esquire and William Rogers Esquire. Chief clerk: J Mallett." He looked up at me. "Your concern, I take it, is that Willoughby is not acting alone. He talked of his superiors, so it seems that his orders are coming down from on high. But why are you so certain that there is any connection with his colleagues at the police office? He could be working with anyone – any crew of rogues."

"And I pray that it is so," I said. "I have no qualms about dealing with thieves and robbers. But you know as well as I that blackmail – particularly protracted and successful blackmail, as we have here – demands a level of planning and patience entirely beyond your average villain, or even a rum cove. They want a quick profit and an even quicker escape." Wontner nodded. "And Willoughby met Edward Brigstock in Scrle's at eleven this morning, so he had permission from someone to be out of the office during court hours."

"So you suspect that the scheme is being controlled from the Hatton Garden police office. Why have you not gone straight to Mr Conant with your suspicion?" He looked at me. "Do you suspect him of being involved himself? Or of knowing about it already but preferring to protect his colleagues?"

If I had thought to hide my deepest concerns from John Wontner, I had been mistaken. "I will admit that for a fleeting moment I considered it. And you know what it costs me to say that." Wontner nodded. "After all, if one magistrate can abuse his office, so can another. But John Conant is made of better stuff than most men – let alone than most magistrates – and I would go to my grave swearing to his honesty."

"Good," said the keeper. "I agree."

I held up my hand. "Even so, it is quite something for me to stand before him and accuse even a court clerk – let alone a chief clerk or a magistrate – of being involved in blackmail. Who knows how he will react to such a suggestion?"

Wontner smiled. "Why, I should think you do, Sam. You have worked closely with the man for years. He trusts you implicitly, and has given you responsibilities and instructions far beyond the norm for a constable. Are you honestly telling me that you cannot predict what he will do if you go to him with this information? After all, it is not gossip or supposition: you know that a clerk at a magistrates' court is involved in blackmail." He waited, and I nodded in agreement. "You know also that this clerk has superiors whom he has to consult, and you suspect – fear – that they may be his superiors in Hatton Garden." He paused. "Perhaps even a magistrate." Another pause, and I nodded again. "You have often told me that one of the things you most admire about Mr Conant is his realism."

"That is so," I said. "He does not turn his face from the harsh truth of his job."

"Does Mr Conant always agree with the other magistrates at Great Marlborough Street?" asked Wontner.

I shook my head, laughing at the very idea. "Indeed he does not. He tries to be discreet, but sometimes his exasperation shows."

"So..." said Wontner slowly.

He was right, of course. I was not dealing with a timid virgin who thought the world a fine and shining place. Mr Conant was an experienced magistrate who knew the worst things that human beings could do, and who knew precisely because of that experience that magistrates were not always the wisest of creatures. Being confronted with a theory that included the possibility of a corrupt magistrate would upset him, but not horrify him.

Although I left Newgate with purpose in my step, I found my spirits sinking as I neared Great Marlborough Street, and by the time I was in Poland Street my usual smart pace had slowed to a dawdle. When I reached the corner

I stopped and looked along to the police office in the hope that one of the message lads would be waiting with a desperate call to action and hare along to deliver it to me, thus preventing me from ever reaching my destination. But of course no-one was waiting, and I had no choice but to head for an uncomfortable interview with Mr Conant.

Tom Neale was standing behind the counter in the front office, while George Cooper – the gaoler – was leaning on it. They were laughing at a shared joke, but soon stopped when they saw my face.

"You look like you've lost a shilling and found a six-pence," observed Tom.

"More like lost a crown and found a farthing," added George. "What on earth's the matter, Sam?"

It was tempting to tell them of my concern, if only to hear them say how ridiculous it was, but it seemed wrong to blacken a man's name on only a suspicion. Enough reputations were being damaged without my trampling on another. If it turned out that not only a court clerk but also a magistrate were involved, Tom and George's outrage would be heard all the way to Hatton Garden, and there was time enough for that.

"Is Mr Conant in his rooms?" I asked.

"Aye," said Tom. "He finished hearing the charges about twenty minutes ago. He's in a jovial mood, if that's any comfort."

I knocked lightly on the door of Mr Conant's dining room and he called me in. He was standing at the table, pouring a drink.

"I was just about to..." he waved the decanter at me. "Would you care to join me?"

"Thank you, sir, that would be very welcome."

He poured two glasses, handed one to me, and indicated that we should take the armchairs.

"Your good health, sir," I said, raising my glass to him.

"And yours, Sam." He took a sip and smiled at me. "Actually, this is fortuitous timing. I have had some welcome news, and it is always more pleasurable to share happy tidings."

"The men downstairs said that you were in a jovial mood."

"Did they indeed?" He smiled wryly. "One of the dangers of working in a police office is that you are surrounded by men who are trained to notice things."

"And what is this welcome news, sir?"

"Lily turned twenty-one a few months ago, as you know." I did know: Conant's daughter was a favourite with everyone at Great Marlborough Street, and as Lily's birthday celebrations had gathered pace Martha had quizzed me every night for details of the latest preparations. I will confess that I was mightily relieved when the grand occasion came and went and all talk could cease of flower arrangements and evening menus and dancing shoes. "Her age makes little difference to Lily," said Conant, "and none at all to me. But her aunt – her late mother's sister and a remarkably silly woman – has taken it into her head that if Lily is not married off soon, all hope will be lost." He shook his head.

And I knew what the magistrate would not admit even to himself: that he secretly hoped that his bright, vivacious daughter with her ready smile and her thousand small concerns for the comfort of her papa would never find a man to marry. His son had taken a wife some years earlier and had already produced four children, so any desire Conant might have to bounce a grandchild on his knee could be satisfied several times over, without losing the daily companionship of his beloved daughter. The magistrate continued. "To this end, Maud – my sister-in-law – has been parading what she considers to be eligible young men before Lily. Each has been more ridiculous than the last, with their leather breeches and cravats so stiff they can't even see their own boots. None was any threat..." Conant stopped and looked at me as he realised what he had said. I kept my face as bland and expressionless as I could. "Lily showed no interest in any of them," he corrected himself quickly, "until a couple of months ago, when she started talking about a fellow called Cranfield. Son of a surgeon and heading that way himself – sounded a steady sort, to be honest, and I did wonder whether I should be expecting to hear from him. And then this noon, Lily came here to tell me that it's all off. Cranfield's in disgrace over something or other and his family has packed him off to distant relatives up in Scotland."

"Was your daughter upset?" I asked, as it would sadden me to think of Lily with a broken heart.

"More puzzled than upset, I would say," replied Conant. "Over the years I have probably confided in her more than I should, so she is not as naïve as many of her acquaintance. Although she can't be certain, she did venture the possibility that there might be another woman in the story."

"Then Mr Cranfield is a fool," I said, and I meant it.

"And I am grateful," replied Conant. "If he is a rake, better we find out before the wedding than after." He stood and went to the decanter again, returning with it to refill both our glasses. "But you did not come up here to find out about Lily's social whirl or my lucky escape, Sam. What is it you wish to discuss?"

The magistrate sat silently as I described Edward Brigstock's meeting at Serle's; I ventured no opinions but kept to simple facts until the end of my tale. "When I realised the possible implications of what we had found," I said in conclusion, "I went to see John Wontner at Newgate. He is a steady, clear-thinking man, with a fine understanding of the delicacies of such a situation."

Conant looked at me sharply. "So you took this matter elsewhere before bringing it to me?"

I swallowed. "I did, sir. I was... uncertain of your reaction to my suggestion that a magistrate might be involved."

"And you thought we might band together – that I might seek to protect one of my own?"

I hung my head for a moment, and then forced myself to meet his eye. "I did, yes. But only for a moment. A brief moment."

The magistrate nodded. "And what did Mr Wontner advise?"

"He advised me to trust to your judgement."

"I should be flattered, I suppose," said Conant, smiling sadly. "Dear God, surely it is not too much to expect a man to honour the duties of his office and keep his nose out of the trough? We are still repairing damage done to the reputation of the magistracy by those blasted Mainwarings, and now this."

I knew only too well the case he meant. At the start of the century, parliamentarian and banker William Mainwaring had served as chairman of the Middlesex bench. He ensured that his own son was elected treasurer, thereby giving their family bank custody of substantial public sums, and used his influence to have the takings from the Haymarket tolls deposited there too. When their bank collapsed they owed the county thousands, but such was Mainwaring's control of his bench that even when he was forced to retire in disgrace his colleagues petitioned the government to grant him a pension from public funds. Although new laws had been brought in to control such 'trading justices', public confidence in the magistracy was still fragile, and I did not envy Conant his current dilemma.

"Will you refer the matter to the Lord Chancellor?" I asked quietly.

Conant sighed. "Eventually I suppose I shall have to." I must have looked surprised, for he added quickly, "Not that I am reluctant to report suspected wrongdoing in a colleague, not at all. If a clerk is abusing his position, that must be exposed – and a thousand times more so if it is a magistrate involved. Rather I am thinking of the best way to proceed with our own enquiries. If we are too hasty to draw down suspicion onto our colleagues at Hatton Garden, will that not alert Brigstock's tormenters?"

I nodded. "I see exactly what you mean, sir. Perhaps the wisest course of action would be for me to see if I can confirm – or hopefully disprove – their involvement, but with an agreed time limit on my enquiries, after which you will take your concerns to a higher authority."

"That sounds very sensible, Sam," said Conant with evident relief. "I shall make sure that you are released from other duties to concentrate on this matter. It will involve some delicate negotiation with Mr Dawson, but I daresay I shall cope." He smiled thinly. "Shall we say a month?"

I agreed, and we both drained our glasses.

CHAPTER TWELVE

Losing on the lottery

WEDNESDAY 10TH MAY 1826

Despite our plans, events quickly overtook both Mr Conant and me. Only a few days after we had agreed that I should make discreet enquiries into matters at Hatton Garden, he called me again into his rooms. Sitting in the armchair by the fireplace, her hands turning over themselves in her lap, was Lily Conant. She smiled sweetly and asked after Martha as she always did, but I could tell from her eyes and her pale cheeks that she was troubled.

"Tell Constable Plank what you told me," prompted her father. He put a dining chair alongside his daughter and indicated that I should sit.

"Yesterday I called on my friend Lucy Cranfield." She looked carefully at me. "I believe that papa has spoken to you of Lucy's brother Charles." She flushed very slightly but then stiffened her back and continued. "Mr Cranfield and I met on several occasions and found that we had many interests in common. He is to be a physician like his father, and has a great deal of determination and ambition, but tempered by a caring nature. I had begun to think..." She looked away.

"There is no cause to be embarrassed in front of Constable Plank, my dear," said her father gently. "He's a soft-hearted fellow himself. But perhaps talk instead about what Miss Cranfield told you."

Lily nodded tightly and continued. "I knew that Charles – Mr Cranfield – had done something to displease his father, because a week ago he sent word that he was going up to Scotland to stay with some cousins, and to complete his medical training there. In short, I was to forget about him. He gave no explanation, and I wondered whether his family did not welcome our... our attachment. I was also angry that he had not been brave enough to face me himself, and that I had been so mistaken in his character." Her father placed a hand on her shoulder and she patted it. "I daresay that I am not the first woman to be taken by surprise by a man's actions."

I smiled at her. "Indeed not, Miss Conant."

"I resolved to put the matter behind me. And then yesterday afternoon I received a note from Lucy, asking – begging – me to call on her. Lucy has always worshipped Charles, and so I assumed that she simply wanted to talk about him with someone else who had cared for him. But instead she told me that she had found out why he had been sent away; she had heard her parents arguing about it. It was not because of our attachment at all. Charles had lost a small fortune – all the money his father had given him for his studies, an inheritance from his grandmother and more besides – on the lottery."

"The lottery?" I was astonished. The public lottery had been going for years, but the hypocrisy of having the government condemn gambling and then run their own lotteries had eventually led to the declaration that the lottery in July of this year would be the last. As a consequence, interest was fierce in what was seen by many as their final chance for an easy profit. Most people who fell for the lottery's lure of easy money were poor and desperate and could ill afford the wager, but wealthy individuals too had been known to succumb to its temptations and it seemed that Charles Cranfield was one such.

"It is just as my father feared," said Mr Conant, looking up at the portrait above the fireplace. "Over a decade ago he gave evidence against the lottery to the House of Commons, warning that it encourages theft and speculation and leads only to loss and disappointment. He also railed against the Morocco men, and yet – ten years later – we are still plagued by them."

"Who are the Morocco men, papa?" asked Lily.

"The Morocco men are called that because they carry Morocco-bound ledgers – and in fact they are just as likely to be women as men," explained her father. "They sell illegal insurance on lottery tickets. If you buy a ticket, you can take out insurance against that ticket not winning, except of course the insurance is not backed by any guarantee and you will have the Devil's own job to claim on it. We see dozens of these charlatans in court every month, and all we can do with them – miserable, exploited creatures that they are themselves – is commit them as rogues and vagabonds."

Lily was nodding in agreement. "Lucy mentioned something about insurance – she did not know what it was, but she heard her father say the word."

"Mr Cranfield's father may have made the wrong decision in sending his son to Scotland," I observed. "I believe that they have declared in Glasgow that they will ignore the ban and run the lottery again next year."

"But at least up there Charles will be away from the influence of those who tempted him." I looked at Lily with surprise. She nodded. "Lucy told me that at least once a week two men would call on Charles at home. He refused to say who they were when she asked him, but once I arrived just as they were leaving, and although they tried to hurry past me, I did see the face of one of them, and I knew him. I thought little of it at the time, but now

I wonder whether they were collecting wagers or this insurance from Charles."

"And who was the man you recognised, my dear?" asked Conant.

"That's the funny thing, as I couldn't imagine what connection there would be between him and Charles. It was Julius Percival."

Conant looked at me with great sadness.

"Is this gentlemen related to Mr Harmon Percival? The magistrate at Hatton Garden?" I asked.

Lily nodded. "His son, yes. That's why I remembered it – the coincidence of Charles knowing two children of magistrates. Julius and me."

After Mr Conant had sent Lily home with promises of following on shortly himself, he stood looking out of the window down into the street. This was his usual pose when thinking deeply about a matter that troubled him, and I knew better than to interrupt him. Eventually he spoke without turning round.

"As soon as Lily told me about Percival's boy, I feared we had found our man." He sounded tired.

"It may all be coincidence, sir," I offered. "All that we know with certainty is that young Cranfield has been exiled in disgrace and that he is friends with the son of Mr

Percival. The other details are not facts but only supposition – we are relying on what his sister overheard and half understood."

"Indeed," said Conant, "but with what we already suspect, does it not seem possible to you – likely even – that Charles Cranfield is being blackmailed, and that this lottery story is simply something he cooked up to explain his spending to his father?" He now spoke so quietly that I had to lean forward to hear him. "Perhaps Cranfield has the same appetites as Francis Brigstock."

We were both silent for a few moments. "If so," I said eventually, "your daughter is safe from him now."

Conant turned from the window. "I have heard rumours that Harmon Percival's financial situation is precarious. He invested heavily in spice crops in the Far East, they say, but harvests and profits are not what he and his fellow investors had hoped. And who knows what a man on the brink of financial ruin may do?" He returned to his chair, passing a weary hand across his eyes, and sat down heavily and sighed. "This latest information has put us both in a difficult situation. If we suspect wrongdoing on the part of a magistrate and do nothing, we are not only condoning his behaviour, but also encouraging it. You know as well as I that all criminals grow in confidence with each day that they remain untouched. But I fear that the suggestion of another scandal might make people close ranks. I doubt Percival would be as brazen as Mainwaring – from what I have seen of the man, he is cunning but essentially a coward – but there is the danger that he might be encouraged to fade away quietly rather than be brought to book for his crimes. His alleged crimes." He corrected himself quickly. "Lily's revelation adds to our knowledge, but I think our plan should remain unchanged: we make our own enquiries, and then, if we are no further forward in a month, I go to the Lord Chancellor with my suspicions."

He stood and so did I, but as I turned to leave he put his hand on my arm. "If you were treading delicately before, Sam," he said quietly, "now you are on eggshells."

CHAPTER THIRTEEN

A ferret in the Compter

THURSDAY 11TH MAY 1826

Martha looked at me appraisingly over the top of her cup. I smiled at her, I hoped reassuringly, and she sniffed. It has never been easy for me to fool her as to my state of mind, and with each year we spend together it becomes harder. She stood and collected the dishes from the table.

"As I see it, Sam," she said with her back to me, wrapping the bread to keep it fresh, "you have a simple choice. You can smile and go to work, pretending that all is well, and we can both worry all day. Or you can tell me now what is on your mind, and we can decide together what to do about it."

She turned and looked at me, her arms folded and her head tilted to one side. I gave up the fight and told her about Lily's visit to the police office – to which she responded, as I had, that the girl had had a lucky escape. I explained Mr Conant's concerns about Hatton Garden, and why he was reluctant to go straight to the Lord Chancellor, and how we had decided on a month's grace period – of which three weeks was now left – for me to make my enquiries.

Martha listened to me carefully, watching me all the while. It is just as well that I am not the sort of man to stray, as I have long suspected that even the most practiced Lothario would find it hard to keep a secret from Martha and her steady brown eyes. When I had finished, she sat down in her chair and leaned back with some satisfaction.

"And I thought it was some terrible dilemma keeping you awake last night." Ah, so she had noticed that too.

"But it is a dilemma, Martha."

She shook her head. "Not at all: a dilemma presents two or more possible routes, whereas with this you have no choice. What you have here, Constable Plank, is an uncomfortable situation into which you wish you did not have to probe – but no dilemma."

She was right. Of course she was right.

"So now I find myself married to a philosopher," I said. "Sometimes I wonder whether teaching you to read was a good idea," and I ducked as she went to pinch my ear.

Just then there was a knock at the door. A scruffy lad stood outside, a note in his hand. I gave him a coin, and Martha reached round me to pass him an apple. He flashed her a quick grin and a "Ta, missus," and scampered off down the street.

"Keep doing that, and they'll learn to write just to deliver their own messages to me," I said as I unfolded the note. "It's from John Wontner at Newgate – he says he has a prisoner he wishes me to meet this morning." I looked up at Martha. "He says it may have something to do with Hatton Garden."

"There – you see. It's the next step for you. No dilemma at all, for a man who knows the right thing to do. Give my regards to Mr Wontner and his wife."

I am usually fond of a long walk, but the weather that morning was so foul – an unseasonably chill cutting wind rushed along the streets and hurled bursts of rain at those unfortunate enough to be outside – that I hailed a coach. The jarvey sat hunched on his bench, his collar turned up high and his hat pulled down low so that only a pair of rheumy eyes was visible. When I told him our destination, he cleared his throat, spat into the gutter, and ventured, "Here's hoping you can get away again just as quick." That made me wonder whether, with the inclement weather, it might be prudent to secure him for the journey back to Great Marlborough Street, and so at Newgate I paid him half the fare and instructed him to wait.

"The horses need tending anyway," he said, glancing down at his animals. "There's a waterman just up there on Giltspur Street, and I'll get a jar myself at the Fortune of War. I'll be back here in half an hour, if that suits."

I nodded, and the coach pulled away. A half-hour would be plenty, as I knew John Wontner would be busy: Thursday is the general removing day for prisoners, when those committed for trial at the Old Bailey are brought to Newgate from houses of correction and gaols across London. And indeed everyone was occupied as I entered the prison; the warder who opened the door recognised me and simply jerked his head in the direction of the keeper's office before returning to his other duties.

The activity in the rest of the prison gave particular emphasis to the calmness in Wontner's office. The eye of the storm, Martha called him, and she was right. I try to keep an even temper myself – I'm not built for fighting, not now I'm in my middle years, and I prefer to steer others away from that course of action – but Wontner was in a class of his own. As soon as I stepped into his room and closed the door behind me, I felt at peace.

"Sam," said Wontner with genuine pleasure as he stood to shake my hand. "You had my message, then." He indicated a chair and I sat. "We're expecting a prisoner from the Borough Compter, and when I read the charge I thought you might like to have a word with him. Given what you said the other day about your blackmail enquiries. He's due soon, and the warders know that we are waiting for him, so if you don't mind..." He glanced down at his desk which, as ever, was covered with papers.

"Of course, John, of course. You carry on; I am perfectly content to wait," I said. As I had tried so often to tell Wilson, a constable's notebook means that no time is ever wasted. I took mine out of my pocket, and leafed back through the recent entries, reading again what I had written and making additional notes and underlinings as I saw fit.

After only five minutes there was a knock at the door and one of the warders looked in. "Mr Johnson, as you requested, sir. Papers." He handed them to the keeper, and then ushered a man into the office. He was about twenty, with a hatchet face and his chin jutting forward in the manner of someone trying to look more confident than he feels. "Stand there," said the warder, pointing to a well-worn spot on the floor in front of Wontner's desk.

"This is the keeper, Mr Wontner. If we warders hear you've cheeked him, we'll take it very personally."

"Thank you, Mr Granger," said Wontner. "You must have upset our Mr Granger," he observed to the prisoner as he looked over the document he had been handed. "Name?"

"Edward Johnson."

"Date of birth?"

"November of 1806, thereabouts."

"It is stated here that you are charged with the black-mail of three gentlemen. Is that correct?"

"Charged, aye." The contempt in the prisoner's voice made the warder take a step further into the room, but Wontner held up a hand.

"Then you are officially handed into my care," said the keeper as he signed the paper and handed it back to Granger with a smile. The warder gave Johnson one last hard look before leaving and closing the door behind him.

"This is Constable Plank of Great Marlborough Street," said Wontner to Johnson. "He is not involved with your case, but is looking into the affairs of a Mr Francis Brigstock." I knew that the keeper was watching the prisoner's face and would tell me of any reaction; from my position, I saw the man's hands, which were clasped behind him, turn white at the knuckles. He knew the name. "Constable Plank, looking at the details of the charges facing Mr Johnson, I see that he is accused of approaching three men on three different occasions. On each occasion, the man has been told that Mr Johnson 'knows his tastes' and that unless he pays over money, those tastes will be made public. If the man demurs, Mr Johnson has then informed him that he will make a complaint against him of committing sodomitical practices in the back of a hackney – with a jarvey prepared to say that both men were present in his vehicle. Is that right, Mr Johnson?"

The prisoner said nothing.

"Are the charges accurate, Mr Johnson?" asked Wontner. "I ask not if you are guilty – that is for the court. I ask simply if the charges I have read are the ones you are here to answer."

"Aye," said Johnson.

"Is one of the alleged victims Mr Brigstock?" I asked the keeper. I was struggling to see the connection between Johnson and my current concerns.

"No," replied Wontner, "but while Mr Johnson was in the Borough Compter, he made the acquaintance of one of my little ferrets." Johnson frowned in confusion; rats were common in prison cells, but not ferrets. "We prison keepers, Mr Johnson, must have eyes and ears where we cannot be ourselves. Certain long-serving prisoners will ease their discomfort by selling us information that they overhear. And the sharp ears of one of our Compter ferrets heard you boasting about how you select your victims." This time the prisoner turned pale and his shoulders sagged; Wontner's information was right.

"Constable Plank," explained the keeper, "when Mr Johnson tells a man that he 'knows his tastes', he is not lying. The victims are chosen because they are known to favour young girls. The threat of accusing them of sodomy is used only on the more reluctant, and it is a clever device. Our courts, as you know, take a dim view of sodomitical practices, but a more tolerant one of men who prefer the opposite sex. Even very young girls."

Johnson's face flushed.

"And you, Mr Johnson," I asked mildly, "do you prefer very young girls?"

The revulsion in his eyes as he turned to look at me was not feigned. "I do not, no."

"How, then, have you become involved in this matter? How do you know which gentlemen to approach with your threats?"

Johnson looked pleadingly at Wontner, who held up his hands in a gesture of surrender. "This is not a court of law, Mr Johnson – I am no judge. We are simply helping Constable Plank with his enquiries, and noting your helpful co-operation here on your papers. You are under no obligation to answer any questions, but..." He indicated an open folder on his desk.

Johnson's sharp eyes narrowed as he considered the implications. Those who live in daily expectation of arrest soon learn the value of a good word from those in charge.

"I get my instructions from a clerk."

"Mr Willoughby of Hatton Garden?" I asked. The prisoner looked astonished. "Mr Willoughby has been known to us for some time," I said. "What we have yet to discover is how Mr Willoughby knows who to target – how he knows which gentlemen are fond of these particular... services." I left a deliberate pause. "There is no escape for Mr Willoughby, of course – we are allowing him to continue only so that we can gather further evidence against him, and his every movement is being watched and noted. Any protection or reward he may have promised those who work for him will come to naught, I am afraid." I glanced at Wontner.

"Of course, Constable Plank, if anyone were able to point you to the source of Willoughby's knowledge, then that person would feel the full gratitude of..."

"Of John Conant Esquire, magistrate," I finished grandly.

We both looked at Johnson. After a few moments, Wontner went to close the open folder on his desk, and the prisoner said, very quietly, "A jarvey. There's a jarvey who tells him who to approach. I don't know his name, but he's a jarvey."

CHAPTER FOURTEEN

Four hands

TUESDAY 16TH MAY 1826

Ever since I had told her about Marwood's lodging house, Martha had quizzed me each evening about who had been observed going to Harrison Street and what I planned to do about making them pay for their depravity. She had mentioned the name of Marwood to Alice, and the poor girl's petrified reaction was all the confirmation we needed of the woman's vileness. By mid May Alice had been with us for about a month, and although she remained cautious and quiet around me, I often heard giggling and chatter when she and Martha were alone together, which showed me better than anything that she was healing.

As I walked into the front office of Great Marlborough Street that morning, the office keeper Thomas Neale beckoned me over.

"Your young house-guest," he said, "I take it she's still looking for somewhere to live on a permanent basis?"

"And the sooner the better," I replied. "Martha grows fonder of Alice and little Martha by the day, and already I dread separating them." What I didn't tell him was that I too would miss them. Sometimes, when Martha and Alice were preparing the evening meal, the milk-scented baby would be deposited on my lap, and with her face turned toward mine and a tiny hand curled around my finger, she seemed to know that I was the closest thing to a father that she would be meeting for a while.

"Well, I've been asking around. Do you know the Blue Boar in Holborn?"

"The coaching inn? Aye," I nodded.

"The innkeeper, George Atkins, is an old friend. His wife has just had their sixth, and his mother lives with them. The old lady is a bit frail and forgetful, but no trouble really. What they want is a girl to live in, to help with the baby and the other little ones, and to keep an eye on the old lady. When I mentioned Alice, George said there was plenty of room for her baby too – if she's looking after one baby, she might as well have two, is how he put it. It's a reputable house, Sam, I can vouch for that."

I grasped his hand in gratitude. "It sounds just the job, Tom – just the job. I'll go round to see Mr Atkins this afternoon."

"Mind your back!" I pressed myself against the inside of the archway as a coachman manoeuvred his horses and carriage past me into the courtyard and pulled them to a halt. The four horses steamed and stamped on the cobbles, and the footman jumped down off the footboard and rolled his neck to stretch it as he walked to the door of the inn. Two ostlers jogged over, nosebags slung over their shoulders, to take care of the horses.

"Where can I find Mr Atkins?" I asked one of them.

"Kitchen – over there," he jerked his head towards the corner of the courtyard while he reached up to take hold of the horse's bridle. "Steady, now – steady." He released the horse from its harness and walked it over to the trough.

The Blue Boar was a successful coaching inn, that was obvious. Its location was excellent, and judging from the noise of voices and slamming doors most of the rooms in the gallery and attic surrounding the courtyard were in use. A few lodgers were leaning on the balustrade, observing the activity below, and piles of boxes and sacks and luggage sat at the four corners of the courtyard, waiting to be loaded. I made my way to the kitchen door and stuck my head round it – I know enough of such places not simply to stroll in. Catch a man unawares with a large knife in his hand, and it's likely the last thing you'll do.

"I'm looking for Mr Atkins," I called in. "I've been sent by Thomas Neale – about the new nursemaid."

From somewhere in the steaming interior came the reply. "Ah, Constable Plank, I believe – we've been expecting you. Make your way round to the front, the main drawing room, and my wife and I will meet you there."

I walked back across the courtyard. There the coach that had come in with me had already been turned around and new horses were in harness. The coachman was climbing back onto his perch, still buttoning his breeches. He caught my eye, and gestured to the large clock on the wall of the inn, which stared down over the courtyard like an all-seeing eye.

"No peace for the wicked, eh, constable – barely time for one pint in and the same out again!" He cracked his whip high over the horses' haunches, and I stood aside to let the carriage roll out under the archway and turn onto High Holborn.

Given the time – just before two – it was not surprising that the drawing room was all but empty. Those who had stopped at the inn for a midday break were once more on their way, and those who would be resting here for the night had yet to arrive. I settled myself in a comfortable chair by the window, and had been waiting only a minute when the innkeeper and his wife came in.

Thirty years as a police officer, and twenty-five of them as a married man, have taught me that it is all but impossible to predict what kind of wife a man will choose.

I would go so far as to admit that, were you to line up twenty men on one side of a room and their twenty wives on the other, I would not be able to match up more than four or five correctly. I daresay it all depends on why a man is taking a wife, whether it is for companionship or for mothering (of himself or his children), for appearance or for the bolstering of his own reputation. For myself, I fixed on Martha because once I had seen and spoken to her I simply could not conceive of living happily without her. But I am completely confident that among those twenty couples – or even fifty – I would have not the slightest difficulty in matching Mr Atkins to Mrs Atkins.

In shape and height, they were of a piece: both tall and spare and angular, both dark-haired and dark-eyed. They were dressed alike, in plain sturdy clothes protected by long canvas aprons, with black boots on their feet. As they stood side by side they looked more like siblings than spouses, and the illusion was complete once they started speaking.

"Constable Plank," he began.

"We are so pleased to welcome you," she continued.

"Here to our home," he finished, and they both indicated the drawing room with a sweep of the arm before sitting down, in unison, on a small sofa opposite my chair.

"We understand," they both said and then laughed. Mrs Atkins put a finger to her own lips and nodded to her husband. He continued alone. "When you marry young, and then work together all day and lie together all night, you grow alike and learn each other's thoughts and ways. Is that not so, my dear?" He looked at his wife, and she put her finger to her lips again. He took that hand in his and kissed it. "You should speak, my dear, otherwise the constable will think that you are frightened of me." And they both hooted at the very suggestion.

I found myself smiling along with them, for who could resist such good humour.

"I understand from Tom Neale that you are looking for a nursemaid to help with your little ones, " I said.

They both nodded vigorously. "We are blessed with six," said Mrs Atkins, "but between us we find that we have only the four hands." They both held up their hands, and roared with laughter – it was obviously a long-standing joke. "Two short, you see!"

"The young lady you are recommending, constable – does she come equipped with the standard two hands?" asked the innkeeper mischievously.

"She does indeed – and with a good and willing heart," I said. "But before you agree to take her, you must know the whole story." The pair looked at me seriously, and I told them of how Alice had come into my home, and that she was seeking a place that would take not just her, but also little Martha.

"The poor girl," said the innkeeper's wife, looking at her husband. "Life without a good man at your side must be bleak indeed. Although a coaching inn is a fine place to meet someone..."

"My wife the matchmaker," said Mr Atkins indulgently. "The only difficulty I see is with the arithmetic. We now have six hands, to be sure, but seven children, counting Alice's baby."

"But with your mother, my dear," suggested his wife. "She may be a bit slower these days, but surely she counts as one hand at least."

"Perfect – seven hands, seven children. Constable Plank, you have solved our equation, and for that we are grateful."

As I left the Blue Boar, thinking to myself how pleased Martha would be at the solution I had found, I felt the first drops of rain. I looked up at the sky, and from the rolling grey slate of the clouds I knew we were in for a downpour. Just then a hackney drew up and the jarvey called down to me. Ordinarily I would have refused, but I was tired and certainly did not fancy a soaking.

"Oxford Street," I said, as the rain started falling in earnest. "Just where it crosses Regent Street." On such an evening, he would be sure to pick up another fare near there.

The jarvey nodded and so I pulled open the door and climbed into the coach, which seemed filled with a strong aroma. I looked around me to see whether someone had left behind a dish of food or a bunch of flowers that could account for it but there was nothing, and so I leaned back and closed my eyes. I must have dozed a little, and woke with a start when the hackney came to a halt and the jarvey rapped on the door. I climbed out and paid him, and he raised his whip in salute before setting off.

Thankfully the rain had all but passed. I turned up Regent Street and marvelled at the sight of the spire of All Souls' silhouetted against the sky, like an arrow to Heaven. As I reached home, I could hear Martha and Alice laughing in the kitchen, no doubt admiring the baby's latest smile or gurgle. And indeed Martha was cooing down at the baby in her arms while Alice peeled potatoes at the table. All three looked up at me as I came in.

"You're early, Sam – your dinner's not quite ready," said Martha.

Alice stood and wiped her hands and then came over to help me off with my coat. As she folded it over her arm, she gave a cry of alarm.

"What is it, Alice?" I asked. She said nothing but held out my coat with trembling hands.

Martha stood and put the baby in the crib that we had fashioned out of a drawer and our softest blanket. She walked over to Alice, quietly and steadily as though approaching a nervous animal. "Tell me, Alice, my dear," she said in a low voice.

"The same scent," whispered Alice. "On the coat. It's his scent."

I took my coat from her, and saw on the back a greasy stain. I sniffed it and then held it out to Martha. She sniffed and considered. "The chemise," she said suddenly. "When Alice first came here."

She was right. "It's from the coach," I said. "I noticed a strong smell when I got in; there must have been something on the seat and I leaned against it."

"Could you ask the jarvey who was in the coach before you? Did you take the number of the coach?" I shook my head. "Can you remember anything in particular about it? Or the jarvey?"

"I was weary..." I said, cursing myself. Usually it was second nature for me to notice these things, but now, and just when it mattered, I could recall nothing.

Martha squeezed my arm. "Never mind," she said. "Perhaps we can learn something from the smell. It's very unusual."

I nodded. "Aye – that could be helpful. And I do know someone who might be able to identify it for us." I looked over at Alice, who was still shaking. "But for now, I shall put this outside." I took the coat and folded it so that the stain was protected, and then left it outside the back door.

Once it was out of sight Alice calmed a little, but it was obvious that very unpleasant memories had been awakened.

CHAPTER FIFTEEN

The wall of pictures

WEDNESDAY 17TH MAY 1826

Wilson reeled from me as I held the stain on the coat under his nose, flapping his hand to clear the air. "Dear heavens! What on earth is that dreadful smell?"

"It's plain to see that you're no Bond Street beau," I replied as I folded the fabric again. "That, young sir, is a scented pomade, used to style gentlemen's hair. Quite what sort, and from where, and sold to whom, well, that is our errand today."

On the way I explained how the stain had been made, and Alice's reaction to it.

Wilson shook his head sadly. "Thirteen years old when a man did that to her. That's a baby having a baby. Our Janey is thirteen, and she still plays with dolls. If a

123

man ever..." He couldn't finish that particular thought. "Where are we headed, then?"

"This pomade – distinctive, would you say?" I asked.

"If by distinctive, you mean disgusting..."

"By distinctive I mean unusual – the sort of smell you would recognise if you smelt it again." I caught Wilson's arm to stop him stepping out into Piccadilly, and a brewer's dray rattled past. "Now I've smelt it twice: once on Alice's garments, and then again in that hackney yesterday evening. And I know just the man to help us."

When I was a young man – before I became a constable, before I spent an unhappy few months as a runner, even before I met Martha – I was a barber. Well, not a barber, but apprentice to a barber. And quite a dab hand at it too, when Jack Rowley would let me take hold of the scissors and razor and practise – either on him, or on an old and trusted customer who would get a free shave and haircut in exchange for letting me learn. Jack was long gone now, but his shop had been taken over by another barber, and this man was hell-bent on bringing his business bang up to date.

Geoffrey Manley's shop was not easy to spot; that was the idea of the place. You had to be in the know to get the address, and even more in the know to be granted admittance. Leaving the bustle of Jermyn Street behind us, I led Wilson down a narrow lane connecting Duke Street and Bury Street. Above us the buildings leaned toward each other, forcing out even the meagre afternoon light, and pigeons cooed and flapped as they settled in alcoves and on ledges. Halfway down the lane was a plain black door, and I knocked twice on it. Footsteps ran downstairs on the inside, and a young lad of no more than ten peered round the door.

"Tell Mr Manley that Mr Plank is here to see him, and requires his help," I said, and the door was closed in our faces and the footsteps disappeared upstairs again. A moment later we heard a cry of "Quickly, quickly, Morris – Mr Plank is one of our very dearest friends!" and the lad reappeared, all but pulled us inside, and, wide-eyed, beckoned us to follow him upstairs.

Now I knew what to expect, but Wilson, well, I am quite sure he had seen nothing like it before. Standing in front of a large mirror fixed to the wall was a high wooden chair. Flanking the chair were two more tall mirrors on wheels, positioned so that whoever was sitting in the chair – empty at the moment – would be able to see himself from all angles. A side wall of the room was fitted with shelves from floor to ceiling; on the upper shelves were dozens of wig stands, each topped with a wig – from the simple to the ornate. On the lower shelves were bottles and jars and pots of all shapes and sizes and colours. And on a small wheeled table pushed against the shelves was an array of barber's tools laid out on a linen cloth like surgical instruments – scissors, razors, brushes, combs and clips. But what caught the eye was the other side wall. Every inch of it was covered in drawings – some original, some pages torn from publications, some coloured, some mere pencil impressions. And these drawings showed men's hair. Every style and fashion imaginable. Some faces I recognised – there was Napoleon, and there his arch-rival the Duke of Wellington, and above them were the actor Edmund Kean and (I think) the painter John Constable. It wasn't a planned display as in a gallery; rather, it was a vertical scrapbook, with new additions simply pinned over the old ones.

Standing in the middle of the room was my friend Geoffrey Manley, and he rushed over to greet us. "Mr Plank, Mr Plank – what a very great pleasure to welcome you once more to my humble premises!" He beamed and shook my hand warmly. "And this strapping fellow, gaping in admiration – who is he?"

"Mr Manley, this is my fellow constable William Wilson." The two shook hands. Manley looked up at Wilson and smiled coyly. The two made an odd pair: Wilson, often the tallest in any room anyway, simply towered over Manley, who was the smallest, neatest, most dapper man you could ever hope to meet. His clothes were plain and unadorned in the fashion currently affected by the most expensive tailors, with the black fabrics as dark as midnight and the white ones as bright as fresh snow. His hands were delicate, with long fingers and carefully shaped nails. And of course his whiskers and hair were the most carefully tended of all, with every trace of grey expertly hidden and every sign of untidy growth ruthlessly removed. Manley waved his arm to indicate the whole room.

"I see you are admiring my decor, Mr Wilson," he said teasingly. "The wigs, alas, are no longer in favour, but I keep them anyway – they remind me of certain beloved people, and preference comes and goes. Who knows whether they might be called for again one day? And this is my wall of ideas. Somewhere on here you will find every shape of head, every slant of eye, every colour of complexion, so no matter who climbs up into my chair," Manley patted the seat of the chair, "I will know what will suit him. Not that they always listen, of course! There are always those who think that an artichoke can be transformed into asparagus with the simple cutting of hair, is that not so, Morris?"

The young lad standing by the door nodded vigorously. "Indeed it is, sir, Mr Manley, indeed it is."

Manley beckoned the boy over and put a hand on his shoulder. "This is Mr Plank, Morris. He is a constable – do you know what that is?" Morris looked up at Manley but said nothing. "Hmmm – perhaps I do not want to know whether you know about constables. But if you are a bad lad and do something wrong, Mr Plank or perhaps

Mr Wilson will be sent to catch hold of you and put you before a magistrate, who will send you to prison, or to Van Diemen's Land. And in neither location, Morris, will you be happy. So what must you do?"

"I must be a good lad, Mr Manley," replied Morris.

"My sister's youngest," the barber explained to us. "None of my own, of course. And you are doing well, Morris – very well indeed. He has even learnt to call me Mr Manley at work, and not Uncle Geoffy as he does at home." Manley winked at his nephew. "But enough of this jollity. You have need of my help, Mr Plank?"

I handed over the coat and explained why it had excited my interest. The barber took the garment and walked over to the window to hold it up to the light. He rubbed the greasy stain between his finger and thumb, and finally put the coat to his nose and breathed deeply.

"Definitely pomade, Mr Plank – but you don't need me to tell you that. Which pomade, now that is your real question, is it not?"

"That, and who might use such stuff – a type of man, perhaps."

"The first is simple to answer; the second, rather harder." Manley draped the coat over the back of the tall chair and walked over to the shelves. He passed his hand across the display until he lighted upon a small, round, white china pot, about two inches across. He took off the lid and smelt it, nodded, and handed it to me. "As I thought. Our starting point."

I sniffed the substance in the pot; it was similar to our stain, but not an exact match. Manley passed me the lid of the pot. On it was a drawing of a bear in chains, and the wording 'James Atkinson's Bears Grease'.

Wilson looked over my shoulder. "Bears Grease?" he asked. "For bears?"

Manley barked in laughter. "Not for bears, my dear fellow – made from bears. Surely you've heard of the bear of Gerrard Street?" Wilson shook his head. "Twenty odd years ago, James Atkinson came down from somewhere up north," the barber, a Londoner to his bootstraps, waved his hand dismissively to indicate anywhere outside the metropolis, "with a tame bear. He set up shop in Gerrard Street, selling fragrances and rose-scented bear grease balm. To advertise his arrival, and – I suspect – to intrigue the bon ton, he put that bear outside his shop every day. That said, it is a fine balm, and very popular. I doubt there is a dandy in London who does not use Atkinson's balm occasionally – the man has made a fortune from the stuff."

"But our stain is not this pomade, is it?" I asked.

Manley thought for a moment. "Originally, yes. But some gentlemen prefer to tailor their scent – to add their own signature, if you will. As an educated guess," the barber twitched his nose over the coat again, "I would say that this is Bears Grease with the addition of cloves."

"Cloves?" repeated Wilson.

Manley nodded. "Very pungent, the clove. A spice from Penang, I believe."

I handed the pot of pomade back to Manley. "You have been a great help, my friend."

The barber swept low in a ridiculously overblown bow, and we both laughed. "For you, Mr Plank, no favour is too great when the debt is so large."

"What did he mean, about a debt?" asked Wilson as we were walking away down St James's Street.

"Mr Manley and I were apprentice barbers at the same time – in premises in the same street – and we struck up a friendship. Although you would scarcely believe it now, his background and mine were similar; my father was a lighterman, and his a deal porter. He's worked hard to conceal his humble beginnings." I glanced across at Wilson before continuing. "As you might have guessed, Mr Manley's preference is for the company of men, although I understand that he keeps his desires to himself these days – and a certain, well, flamboyance is not out of place in his profession. But when we were young lads, his gentle demeanour made him a target of abuse and worse. I took on the role of bulldog, if you will, and after a few snarls and bites from me, his tormenters backed off. He sees it as a debt; for me, it is only what anyone should do when the weak are bullied."

By now we were walking across Green Park. Wilson was silent, and I wondered whether I had shocked him with my reference to sodomy. Eventually he came to a halt and turned to look at me.

"I was wondering one thing," he said slowly. I braced myself for his question. "How does Mr Manley reach to tend their hair? The seat of the chair came almost to his chest, so when someone is sitting in it, how does he reach their hair? Why not just put them in a chair of normal height?"

"A barber is selling more than tidy hair and a neat chin," I said with a smile. "He is selling a man a vision of what he would like to be. The chair must be high, so that the customer feels like a king sitting on his throne – as though simply going to the barber elevates him in the world. And once the customer is seated, Manley pulls a little stool out from underneath the chair and stands on that. Of course, the chair could be lower and the stool discarded – but then the customer is just a man sitting on a wooden chair, and not a king installed on his throne. On a throne, even with the evidence of all those mirrors around him, an ordinary man will believe himself a king."

CHAPTER SIXTEEN

Grand plans

THURSDAY 18TH MAY 1826

When I had told Wilson of my meeting at Newgate and what the prisoner John-son had said about a jarvey supplying names of possible blackmail victims, he had gone very quiet. Several times I caught him scribbling notes at odd moments, and one evening, as Martha was clearing the plates after dinner and Alice had taken the baby out for a little walk, he explained that he had devised a plan for tracking down the jarvey concerned.

I knew we were in trouble when I saw the tightening of Martha's lips, but he missed the signals. Young men – young unmarried men above all – commonly make two mistakes with women. First, they concentrate on trying to impress women rather than learning to understand them. And second, they imagine that once they have their own wife and home, they will be in charge. With nearly a quarter-century of marriage behind me, I knew better on both counts. Martha's face told me that she was not happy with our plans, and that we would have an up-hill struggle to change her mind. And without her backing, I knew, our plans would suffer.

Wilson blundered on. "It's the only way, Mrs Plank. We've talked it through, and if I'm willing..." Eventually even Wilson could not ignore the gimlet stare with which my wife had fixed him. His voice trailed off, he dropped his hands into his lap, and we waited.

Martha exhaled sharply and looked at us. "As I understand it, there is a jarvey who makes it his business to find out about the gentlemen who frequent establishments where they can find the young girls they seek. He passes on this information to Mr Willoughby, who in turn uses it to blackmail these gentlemen." We both nodded. "What you need to do is find out who this jarvey is." We both nodded again. "Can you not just ask the other jarveys? You have friends in their ranks, surely? What about Jem – Butler, was it – the one who helped you last year with that top hat nonsense?"

"Aye, we do," I said. "But for one jarvey to betray another... If word were to get out, the man would be ostracised, his livelihood gone, or worse."

"I did speak to Jem Butler, as a matter of fact," said Wilson. "Carefully, mind you – not giving too much away. And he thinks my plan could work."

"Your plan to disguise yourself as a waterman," confirmed Martha.

"I'm much more likely to find a waterman willing to talk about this jarvey," explained Wilson. "There's no love lost between them, since the watermen lost their jobs on the river with the arrival of the coaches and hold the jarveys responsible."

"But won't the jarveys know all the watermen already?" asked Martha. "Aren't they licensed? Surely they'd notice a new man turning up."

I nodded. "Each stand has three or four watermen licensed to it, and they wear the number of their license on a brass plaque around their neck. But Jem reckons that most jarveys don't really look at the faces of the watermen – as long as the horses are tended swiftly, and there's a place nearby for a quick jar and somewhere to relieve themselves, that's all that worries them."

"And the watermen wear sheepskin hats, so most of my face can be hidden," added Wilson excitedly. "And a leather apron and rug coat, which I can bulk up underneath to hide my true shape."

Martha leaned forward across the table and held out her hand. Wilson looked a little taken aback but placed his hand in hers.

"William," she said softly, "I am not disputing the cleverness of the plan, nor your bravery in suggesting it. But I remember what happened last time you put on a disguise to gather information. You were so badly beaten. And I feel responsible, because Sam and I had the idea and sent you off into that danger."

We all looked at Wilson's hand as it lay in Martha's, his crooked ring finger a permanent reminder of that incident.

"None of us wants that to happen again, Mrs Plank – least of all me," said Wilson quietly. "But I am a year older and more experienced now. More cautious too." Martha raised an eyebrow.

"And we have made better plans this time," I added. "As I say, the watermen never work alone – there will always be men around. While Wilson is in disguise, the other genuine watermen on his stand will be taken into our confidence. Jem has already suggested a likely location, and he seems to think that the watermen there will be only too happy to take part in a scheme designed to uncover a criminal jarvey. No love lost, as Wilson says."

Martha leaned back in her chair and folded her arms. Wilson opened his mouth to say more, but I caught his eye and shook my head. Martha laughed.

"My husband knows me well," she said. "I know how important this is to you – to you both. And if it helps to halt this despicable blackmail... I also know I can't stop

you, William. Him," she nodded in my direction, "well, I
can make things awkward for him if he steps out of line,
but not you. But what I have learned as the wife of a constable – and your wife one day will learn that same hard
lesson – is that the best thing is simply to remind you that
when you are hurt, those who love you are hurt also. So
you must protect yourself in order to protect them. Your
mother and sisters could not manage without you, William – always remember that."

It was only when I saw the small smile on her face as she
looked from Alice to Wilson later that evening that I realised what my wife had in mind.

    After several weeks of good food, a warm bed and –
most importantly – loving care from Martha, the young
mother had lost her haunted look. As she leaned forward
to kiss the forehead of the baby cradled in her arms, she
reminded me of a painting I had once seen of the Ma-
donna and child. And Wilson was a handsome lad, a little
clumsy still to be sure, but he would grow out of that and
would inhabit his fine frame with confidence. The baby
– little Martha – started to snuffle, and Alice looked
around for the tiny cloth dolly that my wife had made for
her. It was beyond her reach, and as she stood to retrieve
it, Wilson held out his hands.

"I'll take the baby for a moment. I'm well practised." I wondered if the comment made him think, as it did me, of the two young siblings he had lost in a fire two years earlier. Alice hesitated for a moment, then passed her baby to him. It was at this moment that I spotted my wife's smile.

I tackled her about it as we readied ourselves for sleep. "I know just what you are up to with those two," I said, shedding my clothes and pulling on my nightshirt quickly so that I could jump into bed and savour the pleasure of watching my wife undress.

"I cannot imagine what you mean, Samuel Plank," she said indignantly, although the skin of her neck had the good grace to flush slightly.

"You, Martha Elizabeth, are matchmaking."

She sat on the edge of the bed with her back to me and felt around her head with expert hands, removing the pins that held – or tried to hold – her wayward curls in place during the day. It was an unthinking display that always filled me with a puzzling combination of tenderness and desire.

"Just thinking ahead, that's all." She looked over her shoulder at me. "Stays, Sam." I unlaced her and she stood to shake her nightgown over her head. "Alice is turning into a good little mother, and I'm teaching her to be useful around the house. In a couple of years' time she will be wanting a husband. And William, well, he's a fine young man."

"A fine young man who lives at home with his own mother and several siblings who rely on him," I added as Martha climbed into bed and craftily tucked her chilly feet under my warm legs. "He is in no financial position to take on more responsibility – even if he were willing to bring up another man's child."

"It is not Martha's fault that she has no father," said my wife sternly.

"Indeed it is not," I agreed, "but no more is it our place to push together two people who have nothing in common save that they are both young, unmarried, and regularly fed by you."

Martha said nothing but simply turned away from me. I chided myself: how long does a man have to be married before he learns that the bed is a poor place for reasoned arguments?

I lay awake; I know Alice did her best to muffle them, but the cries of little Martha still made their way up through the floorboards to our bedroom. Unable to sleep I turned my head on the pillow to look at Martha, and found her already gazing at me.

"Mar," I said softly, "we can't go on like this." She said nothing but looked steadily at me. "I'm very fond of Alice, and of course the baby, but we're not their family – this is not their home."

Martha sighed. "I've enjoyed having them here – nice to have a bit of life about the place during the day."

We both fell silent for a few minutes, thinking of what might have been. A house full of children, with a noisy crowd of grandchildren to follow. I reached up and tucked one of Martha's curls behind her ear. She smiled thinly.

"I'll talk to Alice tomorrow," she said. "About the Blue Boar. By all accounts it's a good place for her and little Martha – she couldn't hope for better."

"They're good people, my love. You'll see, when we take Alice. Good warm people, with room in their hearts and their home. You'll be able to visit whenever you like – a coaching inn thrives on visitors, after all. And little Martha will need to know her namesake."

Martha nodded solemnly, and I knew what it would cost her to say goodbye.

CHAPTER SEVENTEEN

A fresh start

WEDNESDAY 24TH MAY 1826

"This can't all be mine!" gasped Alice as Wilson and I loaded box after basket into the coach.

"Maybe not when you arrived," said Martha firmly, "but it's yours now – yours and little Martha's." My wife looked down at the baby in her arms, who in turn reached up towards her. "It's only some old linen and blankets and cooking bits that might come in handy, and a few clothes from neighbours whose babies are grown out of them."

Alice opened the basket that Wilson was carrying past her and looked inside. "And enough food to feed an army!"

Wilson laughed. "Surely you know by now that it's impossible to leave Mrs Plank's house without a feast fit for Wellington himself. I was as slim as a weasel when I first starting visiting, and look at me now." He patted his stomach ruefully.

"Nonsense," said Martha. "You, William, are still growing, and you, young lady, need all the nourishment you can get while you're feeding this greedy little thing here."

With everything finally stowed in the coach, I helped Alice up into it and turned to Martha. She shook her head, and I understood. She bent her head to the baby and pressed her cheek against the little face, then handed Martha to me and I passed her up to her mother before stepping into the coach myself.

"Wilson..." I started.

"You look after yourself, Alice," he interrupted in a jolly tone. "When you've had a few days to settle in, Mrs Plank and I will be along to inspect your quarters, so you'd better get ready. And I hope you haven't sneaked that pound cake into your basket, for I'm parched and gasping for a slice and a cup of tea, if you please, Mrs Plank. Still growing, as you say."

Martha nodded and smiled tightly, and as the coach pulled away I looked back to see Wilson standing with a hand on my wife's shoulder as she watched us leave.

CHAPTER EIGHTEEN

Wilson and the watermen

FRIDAY 2ND JUNE 1826

The watermen's stand that Jem Butler had suggested for our subterfuge was at the corner of Southampton Street and the Strand. "Nice and busy, especially in this hot weather," explained Jem as I sat alongside him on the coach. "Horses – and men – need more to drink when it's dry. And it's near to Covent Garden. Our man knows that the sort of custom he picks up there might well be interested in what's on offer in Harrison Street and the like." He called out a warning as someone nearly stepped under our wheels. "Don't have the sense they were born with, most folk." He glanced over at me. "What on earth are you wearing? There's a foul stench coming from something, and it's not my horses."

I shook my head. "This is what Martha calls my 'man of Wapping' get-up – complete with fish guts on the boots. I thought in case we ran into anyone, it would be better for me not to look like a constable."

Jem laughed, then put out his arm to indicate that we were turning off the thoroughfare and heading up towards the market. As it was approaching midday most of the stalls were packing up for the day, and we had to weave our way between carts and horses, porters and stray dogs, stacks of baskets and piles of boxes, as we headed for the watermen. One of them darted forward to take the horses' bridles as we approached. Jem leaned down.

"Is the new lad about, Ned?" he asked.

If I hadn't been expecting to see him, I would not have recognised Wilson. As he had promised Martha he would, he wore the leather apron and rug coat of his adopted trade, with padding underneath to make him much rounder than usual – he must have been sweating underneath it all. A sheepskin hat was pulled down low over his forehead, and a brass plaque with his licence number dangled over his belly. But the real change was in his gait. Instead of the upright, confident walk I knew so well, Wilson affected a pronounced stoop, with one shoulder lower than the other. And as he came over to the coach, he dragged one leg behind him.

"You'll need a bit of patience with him," said the waterman with a swift wink as Wilson lumbered across to us. "Looked the wrong way one day and a cartwheel went over his foot. He's a bit slow, to be sure, but good with the horses."

"Water for the horses, sir?" asked Wilson, peering up at us.

"Aye," said Jem loudly, for the benefit of anyone listening. "I'm off to the Unicorn for a jar. Check the dark animal's hoof, offside at the back – I think he's picked up a stone. My man can help you."

Jem jumped down off the bench and headed up Henrietta Street. I climbed down more carefully and Wilson and I stooped together over the hind leg of the horse, Wilson running a hand down the animal's shank to make it raise its foot. As we both feigned interest in the entirely healthy hoof, Wilson whispered to me.

"There are three possible suspects. I saw two of them yesterday and one the day before. The watermen reckon they come here at least four or five times a week, and they remembered them because they picked up or dropped off gentlemen accompanied by young girls."

"Not just family outings?" I checked.

Wilson shook his head. "Wrong time of day, and a waterman working here surely knows the difference between a father and daughter and a ladybird and her escort."

I glanced up to make sure that no-one was watching us. "Anything else? Did any of the jarveys mention having gone to Harrison Street? Or the name Marwood?"

"No – although I didn't talk of those names specifically to the watermen, as I didn't want to put words into their mouths."

"Quite right." I must admit that I was impressed by Wilson's foresight. I straightened up. "If these three come here as regularly as you say, you might not have to stay a waterman for too long."

Jem was striding up the road towards us, and the waterman who had greeted us came over to see him up onto the bench and collect his tip. He jerked his head towards the stand, and Wilson dragged himself and his leg back to wait for the next arrival.

"Thanks for your help, Ned," said Jem as he picked up the reins.

Ned touched his forehead. "Disgusting, it is. I've a girl that age myself." His face softened as he thought of his daughter. "Anything we can do to stop him, we're happy to do." He turned to go, tucking the coins Jem had given him into the pocket of his apron, and then looked back over his shoulder. "There is something I've noticed. One of the three we're keeping an eye on, he's always scribbling away in a book. Often wondered why he didn't get a job as a clerk – nice and warm, especially in the winter. I asked him once, and he said he thought the air was fresher outside than in."

I waited until Jem had negotiated the coach back out onto the Strand before I risked distracting him.

"Can you read, Jem?" I asked.

"More than my name, you mean, and my numbers? Books and newspapers?" He shook his head.

"What about other jarveys?"

Jem pulled us to a halt; he had spotted a cart coming towards us having trouble with a nervous horse.

"You're thinking about what Ned said, aren't you?" he asked, turning towards me but keeping one eye on the jittery animal ahead. He tightened the reins in his hand, just in case his own horses should take fright. "About a jarvey who scribbles in a book?"

"I should imagine that it's quite rare."

"He might be sketching rather than writing," he suggested as the driver of the uneasy horse edged his cart past us.

"But that would still be unusual."

"Indeed." The danger over, Jem touched his horses' rumps lightly with the whip and we jolted forward. "Give me a day or two, and I'll bring you a name. We'll find our scribbling man."

CHAPTER NINETEEN

The scribbling jarvey

MONDAY 5TH JUNE 1826

"Gilbert Thorpe," said Martha as though trying the name on for size.

I nodded. "Jem was as good as his word; he called at Great Marlborough Street today after asking a few questions and greasing a few palms. And he says that Mr Thorpe can read and write."

"Charity school like you?" asked Martha, turning a shirt over in her hands, looking for loose threads.

I shrugged. "I assume so – or a patron of some sort."

"A patron, then to end up as a jarvey?" Martha sounded disbelieving.

There was a light knock at the door. "That will be Wilson," I said, and Martha jumped up to get his dish out

149

of the range. "I swear you give that boy more food than you do your own husband," I said as I spotted the thick wedge of pie.

"And when you start growing upwards again instead of outwards, I'll give you bigger portions too," she replied.

Wilson looked rather taken aback, as well he might, when I opened the door and he caught sight of my wife sticking her tongue out at me.

"Come in, come in," I said with feigned weariness.

Wilson shrugged off his waterman's coat and sat at the table, falling on the pie with gusto. Martha and I waited, she smiling indulgently. When he had finished, Wilson leaned back and patted his stomach.

"Thank you, Mrs Plank – that was just what I needed. I get plenty of fruit from the stallholders – at least the bruised bits they can't sell – but nothing fills a man up like one of your pies."

Martha beamed; I've yet to meet a woman who doesn't like to hear her cooking complimented.

"Do you actually have any information for me, Wilson," I asked quickly, "or are you here simply to sweet-talk my wife into supplying pudding as well?"

Wilson sat up straight, blushing a little, and I felt sorry for what I had said. Martha was right; I too ate like a starving drayhorse when I was that age. I sat opposite him and smiled apologetically. "I'm only teasing you, lad.

Mrs Plank will tell me off for it later, you can be sure."
Martha tutted behind me, but her heart wasn't in it.

"I think I know the name of our man," said Wilson
eagerly. "The three did turn up again, as we thought, and
Mr Gresham – Ned – asked each of them where they'd
come from, just making conversation. And one of them
said Regent Square, which is just round the corner from
Harrison Street. I overheard and said something about
wasn't that near the Foundling Hospital and maybe he'd
been visiting there, and the jarvey laughed in a nasty way
and said that children were probably involved, yes. But it
was nasty, the way he said it."

"Did Mr Gresham know the name of the jarvey?"

"Aye, he did," said Wilson. "Thorpe. Gil Thorpe."

CHAPTER TWENTY

Antics and clowning

THURSDAY 8TH JUNE 1826

"What did Mrs Plank say when you told her what we were doing to-day?" asked Wilson as we stood in the back office at Great Marlborough Street, carefully hanging up our smart blue jackets before putting on the watermen's thick rug coats. If I thought the constable's uniform was heavy in the summer, the waterman's was even worse, but with several fingers now pointing at this Gil Thorpe, I wanted to take a look at the man for myself. Neither Martha nor Mr Conant would have been happy with my plan, and so I thought it wise not to mention it to them.

"Mrs Plank," I said, sitting down to tie the sheepskin gaiters over my boots, "does not need to know every detail of my work." I looked up at him. "And you can stop smirking. Bachelors have no right to smirk at the decisions of married men."

"I mean no offence, sir," said Wilson, looking stricken.

"And you cause none – none at all," I reassured him. "The wife of a police constable always has in the back of her mind that her husband may be in danger – I daresay it's the same for the wife of a soldier. And so, to protect Martha, I sometimes choose not to tell her what I am doing. You will doubtless do the same one day, when there is a Mrs Wilson to consider."

"There is already a Mrs Wilson to consider – my mother – and I tell her as little as possible of my work."

I nodded. "And what neither fine lady needs to know today is that the men they saw off this morning looking bobbish have now turned into this." I clapped the sheepskin hat on my head and we both laughed.

Ned Gresham greeted us with a nod when we arrived at the stand on Henrietta Street. Wilson had explained our progress and plan to him the previous day, and he had arranged for one of his watermen to lend me his uniform but to stay in the area, hidden in the market crowds, on hand should we need reinforcements. Just in case we were being observed, Wilson and I took care to play the part of watermen to perfection while we waited for Gil Thorpe to show up. There was no guarantee that he would, of course, but Ned had said that he came by most days, so the odds were in our favour.

After nearly a week on the stand, Wilson knew what he was about. But I was a novice and discovered that, as with most tasks we disregard, there was more to being a waterman than I had realised. After I had struggled to tie a nosebag onto a horse that didn't like the look of me and bit my hand to prove it, I was demoted to carrying buckets of water, and after I had spilled too much of that through being nervous of more horses that plainly thought I was a pretty poor specimen, I was told to stand at the pump to fill the buckets for others. And even then I managed to kick over a full bucket so that it soaked me from the knees down, much to the amusement of the two jarveys who were waiting on the stand at the time. And this gave me an idea.

I called over Wilson and Ned and explained what I was going to do. From then on, I did as much wrong as I could. I dropped empty buckets with a clang, I brought empty nosebags to horses, I pretended to catch my thumb in the pump handle and danced around like a monkey. Ned rolled his eyes at my performance, and muttered to the jarveys about having to put up with "the wife's idiot half-brother".

Word spread quickly, and by four in the afternoon Ned was grinning broadly. "I should have thought of this years ago," he said with a wink as I tottered comically past him, pretending not to notice that there was water trickling from the bucket I was carrying, down my own leg and into my boot. "Give them a bit of entertainment, that's the thing. Best day we've had in months." And he jingled the coins in his apron pocket.

And just as I was beginning to think that I might have to sign up for another day of antics and clowning, Wilson came over to me.

"That's him," he said. "Just come in, with the pair of bay horses. That's Thorpe."

I glanced over at the coach that had just pulled up to the stand. There were no passengers – just the jarvey. Gil Thorpe was a small, lithe man, with darkish red hair and the weather-beaten complexion of his trade. He jumped down from his bench and handed the reins to the waterman who greeted him, but looked past him to me. I made sure that my hat was pulled down low on my forehead.

"I hear you've taken on a simpleton, Mr Gresham," he called out to Ned.

"Not so loud, Mr Thorpe," said Ned. "Not so loud. He's my wife's relation. Well-meaning, but touched in the head."

Thorpe looked over at me curiously. "Come here, my noddy fellow." I walked over to him, looking down at the ground as though shy. "My horses need water and hay, and I need the pot. Here." He dug into his coat pocket and handed me three coins. "Go to the pieman and get me some dinner. Two coins for the pie, and one for you."

I looked down at the coins in my palm as though I had never seen such a thing before, then across at Ned.

"The pieman, Samuel – with the tray," he said slowly. "The pies," he repeated, pointing first to his mouth and then across the market.

I smiled slowly and set off on my errand. By the time I returned, Thorpe was waiting by his coach, talking with Ned. They ignored Wilson, who was checking the coach wheel for any cracks. As I approached, I held out the pie with both hands and broke into a trot of eagerness. And then somehow my feet tangled up in each other, my toe caught on a cobblestone, and as I tried to right myself, the pie flew out of my grasp and landed on the cobbles just in front of the horses.

As we all looked down at the mess, and Thorpe tried to decide whether to laugh or scold, no-one noticed Wilson climbing quickly onto the bench of the coach, picking up the book he saw lying there, and slipping it into the large pocket of his apron.

"These boots are wet through," said Martha as she pulled them from my feet. "And your stockings." She stood up and went to drape them over a chair in front of the range, tossing me a towel.

"I was caught in a downpour," I said.

"A downpour?" said Martha. "How peculiar: we've had no rain at all for days. Just how far away were you?"

I tried to distract her. "That smells good," I said.

"Anything would smell good to a waterman after a hard day on the stand," said Martha.

"How did you...?" I was astonished.

"I didn't – it was just a guess. But I do now."

I sat back in my chair, pushed the book away from me and folded my arms in disgust. "Well, it's all fiddle faddle to me."

Martha dried her hands and lifted the kettle questioningly. I nodded.

"What's got you stumped, Sam?" she asked as she put the cups on the table.

"It's this book that Wilson got hold of – the one from the jarvey. It's a record of sorts – a ledger, perhaps. I thought it might give us the names of some of his passengers, or where he took them, but it's written in cipher."

"Cipher? Hidden meanings?"

"Or maybe just nonsense. Either way, it's not much use to us."

Martha poured the water into the pot and sat down opposite me, pulling the book towards her. She opened it at random, moved her finger down the page as she read, and turned the page to read some more. Then she looked

up at me with a smile. "When you go into Great Marlborough Street tomorrow morning, ask Mr Conant to
send to Miss Lily for this book." Martha took a scrap of
paper and a pencil out of her apron pocket and wrote a
quick note. She handed it me.

"Mr Phillips's Emblems?" I asked.

"That's it," she confirmed.

"Are you sure Mr Conant's daughter will have it?"

"Oh yes: no young lady of quality would be without it.
You'll see. Bring it home at midday and we'll decipher
this together."

CHAPTER TWENTY-ONE

Hidden meanings

FRIDAY 9TH JUNE 1826

I could tell that Martha was excited about our deciphering because she had left the pots unwashed, piling them up on the side, and instead laid out on the table the items we would need. There was the jarvey's book, and two fresh sheets of paper, and her little pencil was newly sharpened. After sending me to retrieve from my coat pocket the parcel that Lily Conant's manservant had delivered to the police office in response to my note, along with my own almanac, she pulled my chair alongside hers and patted it. She took Miss Conant's book from me and unwrapped it, taking care that I should not see the cover. Then she opened the jarvey's book.

"See, here," she indicated with the end of her pencil. "This entry, for example. It says 'Lotus 16 snowdrop'."

161

"It does," I agreed. "And you say that you know what this means? Is it something for gardeners?"

Martha shook her head, smiling impishly – she was enjoying her secret knowledge. She picked up the emblems book and leafed through it. When I tried to peer at it myself, she leaned away from me and held the book closer to her. "Well, I think that it means Thursday 16th February. Was that date a Thursday?"

I checked my almanac; indeed it had been a Thursday. Martha beamed.

"Do another!" I said, partly to test Martha and partly for the pleasure of seeing her revelling in her cleverness.

She turned a few pages of the ledger and checked the book again. "Olive 5 almond – so that's Sunday 5th March?"

I consulted the almanac again and nodded. "Come on then, Mistress Marvellous – show me the secret."

Martha slid Miss Lily's book across to me. I turned to the title page: "Floral Emblems by Henry Phillips".

"It tells young ladies how to send and receive messages through flowers," explained my wife. "So if a suitor sends her a pimpernel, for instance, she knows that he wishes to fix an assignation with her. And the leaves he uses to encircle the flower will tell her the date he proposes. See: the book starts with which leaves signify which days and which months..."

"So that's how you knew that almond was March, and lotus a Thursday?"

"Well, I don't know them off by heart, as I so rarely receive such gifts from suitors," and she nudged me with her elbow, "but I knew where to look up the meanings."

"Thanks to Mr Phillips we can decipher all of the dates. But what about the other notations? On olive 5 almond – Sunday 5th March – it also says 'austerity'. What on earth is that all about?"

"After the days of the week and the months of the year, the book looks at the meaning of specific flowers and plants. And I think the other words in the entries link to these descriptions. So if we turn to – what was it, austerity? Yes, here you go: Mr Phillips says that the plant to signify austerity is Fuller's teasel – related to the thistle, I think. So maybe that entry relates to someone called Fuller, or Teasel?"

"So anyone else who had this book of Phillips's could take the ledger and work out what it all meant," I wondered aloud, scribbling down 'Fuller' and 'Teasel' in my own notebook.

"I suppose so, yes, but you'd have to spot – or be told – that the emblems are the key to it." said Martha. "Let's try another. What else was written on that entry for Thursday 16th February – lotus 16 snowdrop?"

I turned back in the ledger and ran my finger down the entries. "Cold-hearted."

Martha turned to the right page. "Cold-heartedness is signified by lettuce." She frowned. "I can't imagine anyone called Mr Lettuce, can you?" She slid the book of emblems across to me. "See – lettuce."

I read the paragraph she was indicating. "But what if it doesn't always have to be the plant itself – which would be rather limiting – but just something in the description tion?" I suggested. "After all, the ledger is only to jog Thorpe's memory – it's not a legal record. And look: this cold-hearted entry also has a quotation about lettuce, which is attributed to the poet Spencer – a much more likely name for whoever did whatever they did on Thursday 16th February."

Martha smiled. "We make a good team, Mr Plank."

"We do indeed, Mrs Plank. This afternoon I'll hand the ledger and Phillips over to Wilson, and he can do some deciphering. Now you'd better get on with those pots, my sweet rose of Piccadilly."

That afternoon I explained to Wilson how Martha had uncovered the floral cipher in Thorpe's book. "Go through every entry in there," I instructed him, "and write down what you think it means, using the flower book. Not every one will be clear, but if we can unravel enough names and other details, we can take it to Mr Conant."

Wilson sighed but took hold of the two volumes. I could understand his reluctance; at his age I too would have preferred to be out and about rather than sitting at a desk with a book.

"If we're to leave behind the bad old days of the thief-takers, Wilson," I said, "we have to do things properly. No more paying people to give a bad account of someone. With this information written in his own hand, Thorpe will condemn himself."

"Aye, I suppose that's true," said Wilson, sitting up a little straighter.

"But we don't have long; he'll have missed that ledger by now, and given what Mrs Plank and I read in it last night, he'll move heaven and earth to get it back."

I did not have long to wait for that particular prophecy to come true. There is little point in assigning a task to a man and then looking over his shoulder as he completes it and so I left Wilson to his books and went out for a walk. Many of the local shopkeepers and merchants take comfort from seeing a constable patrolling the streets, and several of them greeted me or touched their caps as I passed.

I had just stopped for a tin cup of milk from one of the maids in St James's Park and was heading back to Great Marlborough Street along Piccadilly when I heard raised voices. This is nothing unusual, of course, particularly on such a thoroughfare; the argument was coming from a coach stand just opposite Burlington House and I suspected a disagreement over a fare. I was just about to step in when I recognised the jarvey at the centre of the argument: it was Gil Thorpe. He was disputing not with a passenger but with the watermen, the other jarveys and indeed anyone else within sight.

"A brown book," he was saying loudly. "Like a ledger, a record book. I had it yesterday, when I called at this stand, and now it's gone." He gestured to the empty bench beside him, then stood and opened his coat to show that there was no book in its pockets or tucked into his waistband.

"And I'm telling you," said one of the watermen, "we've not seen your blasted book. Now clear off with your wild accusations of thievery before we call a constable."

I ducked behind a group of onlookers; the last thing I wanted was to be hauled before Gil Thorpe, who was obviously searching for his book by revisiting all the coach stands he had been to recently. It went against the grain for me to walk away from a public disturbance, but with my mind on the greater prize at stake, I slipped into Sackville Street and turned my step towards Regent Street and the office.

Wilson was still hard at work in the back room, several sheets of paper spread out before him, covered with his careful script. He looked up as I came in, dropped his pencil onto the table and leaned back, his hands behind his head.

"Done?" I asked, sitting in the chair opposite him.

"All but," he replied. "Enough, I think, to show what we need."

"Which is?"

Wilson scanned the table and picked up one of the sheets. "Mrs Plank was right about Phillips. With a few exceptions, the entries can be deciphered with reference to the book of emblems and tied to specific dates. As for the other details, the name that Mrs Plank spotted first," he glanced down at the paper in his hand, "Fuller – austerity in the ledger – that one appears quite often."

"What about Spencer – lettuce?"

Wilson checked his papers. "Twice – no, three times. Plenty of other names crop up like that – perhaps four or five times. But two cipher words come up again and again." I nodded encouragingly. "The first is jest. So I checked it in the emblems," he picked up the book and turned to a page marked with a slip of paper, "and jest or bantering is signified by the southern-wood. Sometimes called Old Man."

"So we're looking for an old man?" I asked. "That's not very precise."

Wilson shook his head. "No – the word 'jest' appears far too often for it to be a customer. I think it's more of a pun. Where does our Harrison Street madam hail from?"

"Mother Marwood? Hampshire, I think," I said. "Portsmouth."

"So she's from the south. A southern Marwood."

I smiled. "I think you're right. Which means we can link her to Thorpe. Good work, lad, good work. And you mentioned a second word that you've seen over and over?"

"Aye. Lustre."

"Lustre? As in shine?"

Wilson nodded. "Like this, for instance. 'Furze' gives us April, 'fruit' gives us Saturday, and 22 is the date – so Saturday 22nd April. It then says 'jest', which we know means Marwood, and finally 'lustre'. When it does appear, this word always comes last – and I think it's giving the location of the, well, the encounter." Wilson blushed a little.

"And what do the emblems say about lustre? Which flower denotes lustre?" I asked.

Wilson turned to another page of the book. "Aconite-leaved crowfoot," he said. "Commonly known as Fair Maids of France."

"France?" I said. "Something to do with the Huguenots?"

"I think it's simpler than that," replied Wilson. "We always refer to Marwood's house as being on Harrison Street, but it's on the corner, isn't it?" I nodded. "On the corner of Harrison Street and Frances Street. The fair maids of Frances Street."

"So from this ledger," I said slowly, counting off on my fingers, "we can work out the names of the customers, the dates of their visits, the bawd involved, and the location of the encounters." Wilson nodded. "No wonder our jarvey was so agitated." I told him what I had seen on my walk. "This information is worth a fortune to us."

"And two fortunes to those named in it," added Wilson.

CHAPTER TWENTY-TWO

Accusations and threats

SATURDAY 10TH JUNE 1826

I stood to one side as Mr Conant read Wilson's notes. From time to time he would look at an entry in Gil Thorpe's book, then at the Phillips, and check them against our interpretation. Finally he sat back, took off his glasses and shook his head.

"Very imaginative," he said. "Although I am surprised that you – or Constable Wilson perhaps – recognised the floral references."

I felt myself colour slightly. "Well, to be truthful..."

I trailed off as Conant held up a hand. "Let me guess: the inestimable Mrs Plank."

I nodded.

"Whatever the source of your inspiration, you and Wilson have done a fine job. I think we have plenty to discuss with Mr Thorpe." Conant reached for a blank warrant; his clerk prepared these for him, writing the standard words and leaving space for the magistrate to complete the details of each arrest. "Thorpe, you said – Gilbert, was it?"

"He is known as Gil," I confirmed.

Conant's clear writing filled the space. "And the charge he is to answer is blackmail?" he asked.

"For now," I said.

"You know where to find him?"

"I have a fair idea, and plenty who can help me," I said, thinking of the watermen who had been angered by Thorpe's behaviour.

Conant signed the warrant, added the date and then placed it in the sand tray. After shaking off the sand, he checked the document and handed it to me. "Any other developments?" he asked.

"No, sir – we have laid our trap, but the loss of this book will have unsettled the gang and they may be lying low for a while."

Conant sighed. "And were you planning to tell me about the part you played in obtaining this book? The office downstairs is alive with talk of your adventures in disguise, so I hear." He took off his spectacles and looked unblinkingly at me. "We are no longer young men, you and I, Sam, however much we might wish it. You are my most experienced constable and extremely valuable to me for that reason. I would prefer you not to put yourself into harm's way any more than is absolutely necessary. What if this Thorpe had suspected a trap?"

"It seemed the best way..." I started to explain, but Conant held up his hand to stop me.

"More care in future, if you please," he said. I nodded. "And time slips away, does it not," he continued. "We allowed ourselves a month for our own enquiries, and here we are, what, five weeks later. Thankfully our next step is clear: we shall speak with Mr Thorpe. But then I shall have to take our findings to the Lord Chancellor." I could hear the reluctance in his voice.

"Is your concern, sir, that we will be chastised for looking into the matter ourselves before reporting it?" I asked.

The magistrate shook his head. "No, although I daresay that will happen. My concern is that we will be the only ones to look into it. Loyalty among groups of men is strong, as you know – be they jarveys or magistrates – and the Lord Chancellor may have no appetite for enquiry into one of his own."

"If that is the case, would it make much difference to continue as we are for a while longer?" I suggested.

Conant smiled at me. "It would certainly be remiss of me to ignore the counsel of such an experienced constable, especially at such a fruitful stage of his enquiries. So yes, perhaps it would be wise to continue for the time being. Oh, and one more thing, Sam," he said as I turned to go. "Please pass on my thanks to Mrs Plank for her assistance in this matter. But don't make those thanks too fulsome, or we might have to put her on the payroll."

In contrast to my visit earlier in the week, I made sure to attend the Henrietta Street stand in full uniform to execute the warrant. This time, I wanted Gil Thorpe to know exactly who I was. I arrived just after noon; I knew from my spell as Ned Gresham's idiot brother-in-law that the jarvey was unlikely to show up until mid-afternoon at the earliest, but I also knew that word would spread quickly among the jarveys that a constable was looking for one of their number, and I wanted to accost him sooner rather than later. On my way out of the police office I had dispatched one of the message lads to Wilson's house; he was not due on duty until two, but I knew he would want to see Thorpe's arrest. And in truth, I thought that the jarvey might come more quietly when confronted with Wilson's bulk.

I was sitting on an upturned crate and had just finished the quarter of pie that Martha had packed for me that morning when I spotted Wilson making his way towards me through the market. Like me, he had taken care to shine his buttons and brush his coat, to make himself look as impressive as possible. He raised his hand in greeting. I wiped the crumbs from my mouth, but not quickly enough.

"Pie?" he asked, smiling. I nodded. "Bought, or homemade?"

"Homemade," I said.

"None for me?"

"It may surprise you to hear that Mrs Plank does not rise from her bed every morning thinking of what she can cook for you. If you're acquiring a taste for home cooking, it might be time to think of looking for a wife of your own." And as the words fell from my lips, I realised that Martha was even more cunning than I had thought. By showing Wilson how comfortable married life could be, she was slowly but surely leading him to the altar, although doubtless when the day came he would think it had all been his own idea.

"It seems quite a step to take, just to get homemade pie," said Wilson.

"Quite right, lad, quite right – and not all women are as skilled in the kitchen as Mrs Plank. You've plenty of time before you need to be priest-linked." I stood and straightened my jacket. "Now you go over there, by the pump, and I'll stand here. When Thorpe pulls his coach in, wait until he's down off it, otherwise he could just whip up and leave. Once he's on the ground, I'll approach him with the warrant," I patted my pocket, "and you come up behind him in case he tries to bolt. He's a young fellow and will be nimble."

Wilson nodded and took up his position. One of the watermen greeted him as he went past with a bucket. The stand was as busy as ever, and there was no time for our minds to wander as with each rumble of wheels coming up Southampton Street we craned our necks to see whether it was Gil Thorpe's coach. The bells of St Paul's had just tolled four when I saw a pair of bay horses coming towards us. I indicated to Wilson, who looked at the coach and nodded in confirmation before stepping behind a pile of boxes so that Thorpe would not see him as he negotiated the corner. As agreed, neither of us moved until Thorpe had pulled his horses to a halt, handed the reins down to a waterman and jumped off the bench. I had considered letting him go to relieve himself first, but a man is always more at ease after that and I certainly had no reason to put Mr Thorpe at his ease.

As the jarvey turned to walk towards the Unicorn, I stepped out in front of him.

"Mr Gilbert Thorpe?" I asked.

"Aye," he said. "And you are?"

"Constable Samuel Plank, of Great Marlborough Street. With a warrant for your arrest signed by John

Conant Esquire, magistrate." I handed him the warrant. He took it and turned it over but did not unfold it to read.

"On what charge?" he asked.

"On suspicion of blackmail. Mr Conant is satisfied that he would like to hear more from you on this matter."

Thorpe looked at me for the first time. His eyes flicked to the side, and I was grateful for our forethought; as Thorpe turned away from me, Wilson stepped smartly into his path and the jarvey cannoned into him.

"Come now, Mr Thorpe," he said coaxingly. "Don't make us run after you, or we'll think you've something to run from."

The jarvey shook himself like a dog but made no further effort to get away. He looked up at Wilson and frowned.

"Don't I know you?" he asked.

Wilson smiled, then dropped one shoulder and rounded his back. "Take care of the horses, sir?" he asked, and Thorpe's jaw dropped. Wilson pointed at me. "And you might know him too, if you look a bit closer." The jarvey turned to me and I touched my hat in salute.

"The idiot – Gresham's wife's brother," he said, nodding slowly. "So you've been watching me for a while, then."

"Long enough, Mr Thorpe," I said as we took hold of him, one arm each, and started to walk down Southampton Street. "Long enough."

"Gilbert Thorpe?" asked Mr Conant, looking over his spectacles at the jarvey.

Thorpe nodded, and I jabbed him with my elbow. "You must answer the magistrate – and politely."

"Yes, sir," he said sulkily.

"You may sit," said Conant, indicating the seat across the table from his own. I stayed standing behind the jarvey, and Wilson took up his usual position at the door; occasionally a man would take it into his head that running from the magistrate would be a permanent solution to his predicament, and it was as well to be prepared.

Conant looked down at the papers in front of him. "You have been brought here today, Mr Thorpe, because it is my responsibility to decide whether you have a case to answer." He glanced at the jarvey. "That is, whether there is sufficient evidence to suggest that you may have committed an offence and so should go before the court. Do you understand that?"

Thorpe nodded, then added quickly, "Yes, sir," as he felt me move behind him.

"In recent weeks, my constables have dealt with several..." the magistrate paused as he searched for the right word, "several incidents involving men who have been forced to hand over money against the threat of certain information being made public. Blackmail, Mr Thorpe." Conant looked at the jarvey, who said nothing. "One of the worst forms of extortion, as it calls into question a man's good name. And once lost, a good name is all but impossible to restore. Quite rightly, therefore, the courts punish blackmail severely." The magistrate leaned forward and took off his spectacles. "Transportation, Mr Thorpe. For several years, perhaps for life."

And still the jarvey made no reaction.

Conant sat back in his chair. "Interesting, is it not, Constable Plank, observing the reaction of a man who is accused of a felony," he said, in a conversational tone.

"Indeed it is, sir," I replied. I saw Thorpe tense slightly, which meant that we were starting to unease him.

"Some," and Conant waved one hand in the air as though encompassing a group of people, "protest vehemently that they are innocent. Others," here a wave with the other hand, "cry in remorse for their guilt – or at least for the punishment that awaits them." He turned both palms upward. "But Mr Thorpe, constable, neither protests nor cries. Almost as though he believes he has nothing to fear." He said these last words slowly, one careful syllable at a time.

"Perhaps, sir," I ventured, "he imagines that none of the men involved will come forward to accuse him."

"Certainly the late Mr Francis Brigstock will not," agreed the magistrate, nodding. "And even those who are still alive may not wish to stand in court and explain why they paid Mr Thorpe and his associates. Accusations of sodomitical acts in the back of a hackney are hard to prove, but even harder to disprove. And with severe penalties and ruined reputations at stake, well, little wonder that they pay up."

"If I were Mr Thorpe, sir, I too might feel confident on this matter."

"And so might I, constable, so might I – were that the only matter facing me."

From behind I could not see the jarvey's face, but his hand, lying along the arm of the chair, tightened its grip.

Mr Conant continued. "You see, Mr Thorpe, interesting and diverting though your efforts at extortion have been, that is only the start of things. I believe that you, Constable Wilson, have been reading about Mr Thorpe's other line of work."

"I have, sir," said Wilson, and I beckoned him forward.

"In a most illuminating book, is that not so, constable?" asked the magistrate, holding out his hand.

Wilson leaned past the jarvey, who shrank from him, and handed to Mr Conant a book wrapped in brown paper. The magistrate placed it on the table and took a penknife to the parcel's string. "A ledger, it seems," he said as the book was revealed. "Yours, I believe, Mr Thorpe."

I'll say this for him, the jarvey was quick. With Wilson away from his post at the door, and my attention on the book, he leapt out of his chair, sprinted across the room and hauled at the doorknob. Wilson turned with a yell of anger, but it was too late: Thorpe had galloped down the stairs. Wilson thundered down them after him while Conant and I dashed to the windows.

We saw the jarvey dart across the road and down into Carnaby Street; Wilson was halted for a moment by a passing cart and then took off after him. We waited for about five minutes, only to see Wilson return alone, a disconsolate droop to his shoulders. He looked up at the windows of the dining room and shook his head.

Martha loaded a plate with bacon and potatoes and put it in front of me.

"I had mine earlier," she explained. "I thought you might be out later, when you sent the message saying you had that jarvey in for questioning." She reached across and pinched a piece of meat. "But the rat escaped the trap, it seems."

"He did," I said, "but he won't get far. We've put out the word to the jarveys, and – apart from the few who must be helping him – they won't be keen to see him back at work. Professional pride, Jem talked about."

Martha gestured to the pan on the stove and I nodded, so she ladled two more potatoes onto my plate.

"One thing has been bothering me," she said as she sat down again. "Thorpe's book. It was written in a beautiful hand. A schooled hand. Not like mine, I mean." She blushed very slightly.

Martha's lack of education was a source of shame to her, but for me it was the opposite. When we had first met she was keeping house for her four younger siblings and widowed father as well as struggling to stop him drinking himself to death in his own inn. She could recognise her own name when it was written down, and had a good command of the numbers – she had stock-taking to thank for that – but reading and writing came later. I taught her everything I could, Mr Conant encouraged us both by granting us free access to his library, and her determination to learn – and her aptitude for it – made me proud of her, and of myself for choosing such a clever wife. I reached over and put my hand over hers.

"You, Mrs Plank, are fishing for compliments. And you've landed one: you are absolutely right. It seems that Mr Thorpe is not only swift-footed but also well-educated."

"So why is such a man driving a coach for a living?"

CHAPTER TWENTY-THREE

Sleeping alone

MONDAY 12TH JUNE 1826

On Monday evening I had just lifted my spoon to my mouth when there was a knock at the back door. Martha sighed, for we both knew what to expect: a constable's meal is often interrupted. After handing over a coin and a thick hunk of bread to the lad, Martha returned and passed the folded message to me.

"Shall I put your soup back into the pot?" she asked as I read the note.

"And yours," I replied. "We're both sent for – it's from Mr Atkins at the Blue Boar." Martha's hand flew to her mouth. "All is well with Alice and baby Martha, it says, but Alice needs to see us – both of us – urgently."

We barely spoke on the walk to Holborn – partly because our steady jog-trot left us little breath for anything more, and partly because neither of us wanted to say what we were thinking: that Alice had got herself into some sort of trouble that Mr Atkins could not bring himself to put into writing.

Oxford Street was jammed with coaches and carts – empty ones heading out to collect their deliveries for the morrow, and full ones heading in for theatres and other evening revels. The pavements were likewise crowded with that strange mixture of the respectable and the doubtful that any city sees at dusk, and I kept Martha's arm firmly tucked in mine to protect her from being jostled or – worse – knocked into the road. We made our way through the constant tide of people into Holborn and then High Holborn, and finally caught sight of the sign of the Blue Boar. One of the ostlers was standing in the road, holding up a hand to the traffic to allow a coach to leave the yard before another could enter. Once the manoeuvre was complete, the ostler tipped his hat at us and led us through the arch.

Remembering my first visit, I led Martha to the kitchen and stuck my head round the door.

"I'm looking for Mr Atkins!" I bellowed into the chaos.

A cook looked up from his pots and wiped his brow with a cloth hanging at his waist. "Parlour!" he yelled back. "Supper!"

I backed out of the heat and Martha and I walked round the edge of the yard to the side door of the inn, taking care to keep clear of the stamping, steaming horses being reversed out of their traces and led to the trough. Once indoors, I caught the sleeve of a pot boy rushing past with handfuls of empty tankards and asked him to let Mr Atkins know that we were waiting. A moment later, the gentleman himself appeared and ushered us into the waiting room.

"Two ticks," he said cheerfully. "Give me two ticks to check that everyone is being fed and watered. Talking of which, would you...?"

I shook my head; no need to add our own demands to the list. The landlord disappeared and we could hear him trotting down the corridor.

"He seems friendly," said Martha. "I've met Mrs Atkins, of course, when I've called to see Alice, but not her husband. Aren't they alike? In appearance, and in cheerfulness."

I nodded. "He's certainly in the right job – he welcomes everyone."

It was a little more than two ticks, but Mr Atkins returned about ten minutes later with Alice. She smiled shyly at Martha and dropped me a little curtsey. I rose so that Alice could take the chair nearest to Martha while Mr Atkins and I stood by the door, which the landlord had closed to give us some respite from the noise in the parlour.

"Now, Alice, what is all this about?" my wife asked. "There's nothing wrong with the baby, is there? You're not in any kind of trouble?"

Alice glanced at Mr Atkins.

"No, not Alice, Mrs Plank," said the landlord. "Come on now, girl, out with it. The constable and his good lady have walked halfway across London to listen to you," he said, but in a kindly tone.

"It's my friend, Ellen," started Alice haltingly. "I knew her at – at the house in Harrison Street." We all smiled encouragingly. She took a deep breath and blurted it out. "Ellen's going to have a baby and she's scared to stay with Mother Marwood and her own family won't have nothing to do with her and when I moved here I sent word where I was to the girls in Harrison Street just to let them know that I was safe and now Ellen has turned up here."

Martha and I both looked at Mr Atkins, who nodded.

"Aye, that's the bones of the matter," he said. "This other young lass fetched up here yesterday, in a terrible state. My wife reckons she's about ready to have the baby. We've put her in with Alice and Martha and our youngest, and we can have her here until the baby arrives. But after that, she'll have to find other accommodation." Alice looked up at him. "We're very happy to have Alice here – we don't know how we'd manage without her now." Alice smiled, and Martha leaned over and patted her hand. "But we simply don't have room – and no need of another nursemaid." He looked genuinely sad as he said this.

"But where is she to go, Mrs Plank?" asked Alice pleadingly. "Where can Ellen go?"

Martha stood, and held out her hand to Alice. "That is not your concern, Alice – you did right to tell us, and now Mr Atkins, Constable Plank and I will put our minds to it. Now, gentlemen, you may both return to your business, while Alice takes me to meet Ellen, and to see little Martha."

The clock had already struck midnight, and I was still wide awake in bed. After nearly a quarter-century of marriage, I found it almost impossible to sleep without Martha beside me. I sat up again and thumped my pillow, then fell back onto it with a sigh. Then, thankfully, I heard the back door open, and Martha called up the stairs. Five minutes later, she came into the bedroom and dropped wearily onto the corner of the bed.

"Did I wake you?" she asked, reaching up to take the pins from her hair.

I made a big show of yawning and stretching. "Mmm – what time is it?"

She looked at me shrewdly. "You, Samuel, are play-acting. Have you been lying awake waiting for me?"

"I might have been."

She turned her back to me, but I could hear the smile in her voice. "Makes a change, doesn't it – you waiting up for me."

"So what took you so long? And I hope you didn't walk home alone."

She shook her head. "No: one of the regular jarveys from the Blue Boar was heading this way – Mr Atkins knew him and said I'd be safe with him. Nice lad: expecting his own baby any day now. Didn't charge me a penny – said he was glad of the company."

She wriggled into her nightdress and climbed into bed. I held out my arm and she settled into the crook of it, her head on my chest.

"Oh Sam, you should have seen her. Even younger than Alice. Not a clue about what to expect. That's what took me so long, trying to calm her. Petrified of having the baby. Another girl they knew at Harrison Street had her baby early, and they both died – mother and baby. And Ellen was in the next room and heard it all. Afterwards, she saw the doctor carrying the two bodies out of the house. So we tried to comfort her. Alice and Mrs Atkins told her about what it was like for them, having a baby." She paused for a few moments. "I couldn't do that, of course, having never quite..." I squeezed her a little tighter. She sighed. "But where will she go afterwards, Sam? What can we do?"

I didn't answer – I had no answer – and after some minutes Martha's breathing slowed. That was a problem for another day.

CHAPTER TWENTY-FOUR

The home visit

TUESDAY 13TH JUNE 1826

The next day I woke before Martha. I savoured the comfort of a wife-warmed bed, but I had not slept restfully and something was still making me uneasy. Trying not to move for fear of disturbing Martha, I thought back to what she had said before falling asleep. And then it came to me: she had mentioned a doctor. A doctor had tended the other girl who had died in childbirth, and had then disposed of the bodies.

"And you're sure it was a doctor – not a handy-woman?" asked Wilson as we sat in the police office later that morning.

I shook my head emphatically. "No: Martha checked that with the girl. Apparently Ellen peeped out from her room and saw a man – not a woman – going down the stairs carrying the dead girl."

"So why would a doctor be attending that sort of girl during childbirth? A titled lady, maybe, but a Harrison Street lass..."

"Precisely," I said. "That's what worried at me all night. What would a doctor be doing in such a house?"

"Unless," said Wilson slowly, "unless he was already there. Not called as a doctor at all, but visiting as a customer."

I nodded. "Just a coincidence, perhaps. And as the only man on the premises, it would make sense for him to be the one to carry the body downstairs."

"Although," added Wilson, stroking his chin as he worked through his thoughts, "surely such a man would be reluctant to become involved, if he was there only as a casual visitor."

Wilson was right. Any man there on private business would beat a hasty retreat at the first sign of any trouble. "Which means that he was indeed there as a doctor, in his professional capacity," I reasoned. "But why would a respectable doctor agree to take on such patients?"

"For the same reason that Edward Brigstock was willing to continue paying his brother's blackmailers: fear of exposure. Perhaps this doctor pays for his personal visits to the girls to be kept secret by offering his medical expertise," said Wilson.

I smiled at him. "A very likely explanation, constable. And a very useful one for us: blackmailers and extortioners are not the only ones who can use a man's weakness against him. Time for you to call on a few Harrison Street neighbours, I think, and see if you can get a description of the good doctor. I will ask Martha to see if Ellen can remember anything more about him. There can't be too many doctors making house calls in that part of town."

CHAPTER TWENTY-FIVE

Austerity and ague

THURSDAY 15TH JUNE 1826

Mr Conant shook his head in despair. "What is happening to our country, constable? We were all so optimistic after the war, filled with relief, and determined to honour the heroes who had fought for us. Instead, we have bands of ex-soldiers begging on the streets and stealing from their fellows." He turned from the window and looked at me. "And now you tell me that not only do we have to consider the possibility of a corrupt court clerk and magistrate, but now a corrupt doctor as well. Professional men, all of them – entrusted to serve their community."

I had known he would take it hard. A man who had devoted his life to public service, first in the Navy and now on the bench, Conant believed with all his heart that it was the duty of educated men to improve the lot of those around them.

He walked over to one of the two armchairs near the fireplace and sat heavily into it, indicating that I should take the other. "Come then, Sam – tell me what you know about this doctor."

"According to the busybody living next door to the lodging house in Harrison Street, his name is Stephen Fuller," I said, taking out my notebook. "Fellow of the Royal College of Physicians."

Conant raised an eyebrow. "A proper medical man, then – not someone who learned his trade rolling pills for apothecaries."

I consulted my notes again. "And – as a physician rather than a surgeon – he is not permitted to perform operations or set bones. According to the rules governing licentiates of the College, the duties of a physician are limited to examining patients, diagnosing disease, and prescribing medications." The doorman at the College in Pall Mall had been most helpful, once a few coins had found their way from my pocket to his.

"So it seems highly unlikely that Doctor Fuller was attending the girl at Harrison Street in his professional capacity – even could such a girl afford his services."

"There is something else," I said. "In the jarvey's ledger the word 'austerity' appears often. The floral emblem for austerity is Fuller's teasel. Doctor Fuller, perhaps."

Conant sighed. "You have an address for the good doctor?"

I nodded. "He moved last year to new premises in Savile Street. Rather grand, according to Constable Wilson. The doctor receives patients at Savile Street on Tuesday and Thursday afternoons, and visits them at their homes on Mondays and Fridays." Conant looked over at me. "Constable Wilson has a way of persuading young female servants to answer questions."

"As did you once, I seem to recall."

"Many years ago now, sir – and never with quite as much success as Wilson."

Conant smiled, but his mind was elsewhere. I closed my notebook and waited.

"Is it time to visit the doctor, do you think, Sam?" he asked eventually.

"It is, yes, sir," I said. "And, if I may, I have an idea for that visit."

The doctor's house in Savile Street was, as Wilson had said, rather grand. About a century old, it stood alongside its fellows with the self-satisfied certainty of such premises, two pale pillars flanking the three steps leading up to the front door. Two large windows were on one side of the door and one on the other; if Doctor Fuller were a traditionalist, the larger room would be his consulting parlour and the smaller a waiting room. I tugged on the bell chain and waited.

A neat little maid opened the door – she was probably the one who had been charmed by Wilson.

"Mr Knight," I said by way of introduction. "I have an appointment."

The maid took my hat and showed me into the smaller room.

"The doctor is with someone. I will collect you when he is ready," she said, and closed the door firmly behind her. After only a minute or so, I heard another door open, then the front door, and I glanced out of the window to see a well-dressed young man hurrying off down the street. The door of the waiting room opened, and the maid curtseyed.

"If you please, sir," she said, and held the door ajar. The door of the room opposite was also open, and I went in.

Doctor Fuller was writing some notes at his desk and without looking up he waved a hand at the chair positioned nearby. He was aged about fifty, and was a man of three colours: his hair and cravat were snowy, almost dazzlingly, white; his outfit was sombre black from jacket to shoes; and his face was deep red, of a shade that can be acquired only through many years of over-indulgence at the plate and the decanter. After a few moments he put down his pen and turned to me.

"Mr Knight?" he asked.

I nodded. "I am grateful to you for seeing me at such short notice, doctor. I am at my wits' end. When I mentioned my dilemma to Harmon..."

The doctor held up his hand to stop me. "It is kind of Mr Percival to recommend me. How may I help you, Mr Knight?"

My arrow had found its mark; the doctor and the magistrate did know each other.

I went through the list of symptoms that had caused such mirth at the police office that morning. As luck would have it, one of our regular Covent Garden nuns had been brought in, and she was able to describe the ague for us in some detail. Poor Wilson had gone a bit pale, and I daresay he'll be keeping his instrument in its case a while longer as a result, but it seemed to do the trick with Doctor Fuller.

He nodded and smiled sympathetically. "A clear case. I will write a note for your apothecary. In the past I would have recommended mercury, but silver nitrate is proving more effective, and easier to tolerate." He scribbled on a small sheet of paper, signed it, folded it and handed it to me. "And here is my account." He signed another piece of paper and gave that to me too.

I stood to go, and then turned as though remembering something. The doctor smiled expectantly. "I had thought, doctor," I said hesitantly, "that limiting my – my activity to unspoilt territory..."

"And have you?" he asked. "Exclusively? Absolutely without exception?"

I shook my head sadly. "I try, but it is not always possible to find..."

"Indeed. I sympathise, but I recommend that you do so in future. I myself will touch no – territory, as you put it, that has been conquered by another."

"As at Harrison Street?" I asked. It was a calculated risk. The doctor looked at me sharply. "Harmon suggested that it was reliable," I explained.

Fuller's face relaxed. "And so it is, Mr Knight. So it is."

Just then the doorbell clanged, and there was a soft knock at the door of the consulting room.

"My next patient, Mr Knight. You might prefer to wait here until he is shown into the waiting room."

I did so, and soon I was hurrying off down the street while someone else waited behind that carefully closed door to consult the good doctor.

CHAPTER TWENTY-SIX

Dying with Keats

FRIDAY 16TH JUNE 1826 – MORNING

G ilbert Thorpe did not get far after his escape from us. News of our public arrest of him at Covent Garden would have flashed through the ranks of the jarveys and had no doubt reached the ears of his accomplices, who probably assumed that he would tell us everything to save his own skin. And perhaps, despite my best efforts, Doctor Fuller had detected something unusual about my visit, or maybe Mrs Marwood had noticed that her house was being watched.

Whatever the cause, Thorpe's body was found in Peter Street, half-hidden behind some crates awaiting collection. He had resisted, that much was plain from the bruises and scrapes on his face and hands, but the blade across his throat had had the final word, and determining cause of death would not give the coroner much trouble. Whoever had killed Thorpe had chosen the location carefully: it was only five minutes' walk from our police office, guaranteeing that someone from Great Marlborough Street would be summoned and that Conant and I would certainly hear of the matter. The message was clear: this is what happens to those who impede our business.

Wilson and I looked down at the corpse. The delivery man who had found it had tried to sit him up, in case he was still alive, and Wilson suddenly crouched down and reached behind the body for something that must have fallen out of Thorpe's pocket during the struggle. He stood up, and in his hand was a small book with a scuffed red cover. He passed it to me. It was a very tattered collection by John Keats – not to my taste at all, but obviously much read by its owner.

"Poetry," said Wilson dismissively as he looked down at the book.

"Odes," I elaborated as I leafed through the book. "On a Grecian urn, on indolence..."

"Maybe someone left it in his coach," suggested Wilson.

"Possibly." I turned to the front of the book, and something there caught my eye. In small but perfectly legible writing, familiar to my eye from the ledger, Thorpe had written his name, and address. Gilbert

Thorpe, 15 Bowling Green Lane, Clerkenwell. I looked at Wilson and smiled.

"Shouldn't we leave it for the coroner?" he asked.

"The coroner will concern himself with the body and items found on the body," I said. "This was not found on the body. In any case, I am sure that Mrs Thorpe – wife or mother – would rather hear of this from us, than from some clumsy oaf of a runner from the coroner."

It was gone noon by the time we arrived in Clerkenwell, and as we walked past the Cherry Tree public house Wilson cast a longing look at its door. I realised that my stomach too was rumbling so we went inside for some refreshment. It took a moment for our eyes to adjust to the gloomy interior, but it was pleasant to be out of the heat and the grime. Judging from their clothes, most of the other customers were either labourers from the burying ground nearby or warders from the house of correction down the road. One of these, spotting our uniforms, gave us a curt nod as we sat.

After Wilson had demolished his usual enormous meal at his usual fast pace, we stepped out into the light once more. I seemed to remember that Bowling Green Lane had once been home to a bear garden, famed for its ferocious and bloody contests between animals and even gladiatorial bouts between men, but that was long gone and now the area was a mixture of houses, workshops and stables. The houses were neat and tidy, fairly recently built. I pointed this out to Wilson.

"Always look at where a man lives. This tells us that Mr Thorpe was not surviving on only a jarvey's wage, or that there is another earner or two in his household."

Wilson nodded. "Aye, I couldn't afford a place like this. Although my mother would love it here." He looked over at the mature cherry trees shading the other side of the street.

We stopped outside number fifteen. I checked that we looked neat and sober, and then knocked on the door. A woman in her middle years opened it; mother then, not wife. We both removed our hats.

"Mrs Thorpe?" I said. "My name is Constable Samuel Plank, and I am a magistrate's constable instructed by John Conant Esquire in Great Marlborough Street. I am afraid that I have bad news about your son."

The woman put a hand to her heart. "My son? But I have two sons – which do you mean?"

"Perhaps we should come in, Mrs Thorpe – we can tell you more."

She nodded and stood aside to let us pass.

Mrs Thorpe's tiny front room was immaculate. Two worn but serviceable armchairs were turned to the fireplace. She indicated that we should take them, but Wilson shook his head.

"I prefer to stand, thank you, Mrs Thorpe," he said, and so he filled the doorway while our hostess and I sat down. Mrs Thorpe folded her hands in her lap and looked at me. From the way her chin jutted forward and the tightness of her lips, I could tell she was preparing herself.

"This morning, we found the body of Gilbert Thorpe," I said quietly. She closed her eyes for a long moment and then nodded and opened them again. "He was murdered, that is certain, and we will do our utmost to find his killer or killers." I watched her carefully, but there was no further reaction – she was not surprised to hear that her son had been murdered.

"Did he..." she cleared her throat. "Was it..." She shook her head.

"It was a quick death," I said. "He would not have suffered." No need to go into the details of the titanic struggle that had preceded that quick death; telling his mother would not reduce his suffering and would certainly increase hers. I reached into my pocket for the book of poetry.

"We found this in his possession," I said. "Keats."

She nodded and held out her hand; I passed her the book. "He was so fond of this," she said quietly. "He took it with him every day. For when he was waiting for a passenger, he said – there was plenty of waiting in his job." She lightly stroked the cover of the little volume.

"Forgive me, Mrs Thorpe, but it is unusual to meet a coachman who reads at all, let alone poetry like that."

"But he wasn't always a jarvey, constable. No, Gil started out like his brother, clerks both of them. I was determined my boys would do well in life, despite every-thing, and I made sure that they went to school. John was quicker, that was clear, but Gil was determined. When John left school he easily found a position as a clerk, and then he persuaded Gil to join him. I had my doubts – Gil has always been restless and I didn't think an indoor po-sition would suit him, and sure enough he stayed only a year before leaving to become a jarvey – but John wanted to try. Very close, they were – even with only half-blood shared." She looked up at me with tears in her eyes. "Dear Lord, how am I going to tell John? It will break his heart."

"It will be very difficult, Mrs Thorpe, but you will each give strength to the other. Is there anyone else who can help you?"

She shook her head and clasped her hands until the knuckles turned white. "No: it's just the two of us now." She looked up at me pleadingly.

I leaned forward and placed my hand over hers. "If you would prefer, Constable Wilson and I can visit your son and prepare him." She nodded. "Tell us where we can find him, then, and we will go now." I indicated to Wilson, but he had already opened his notebook and was standing ready.

"He will be at work," she said. "You'll be familiar with his place of work, I am sure. Clerkenwell police office in Hatton Garden – he's a clerk there. John Willoughby."

Wilson started to speak as soon as Mrs Thorpe had closed the door behind us, but I hushed him and we walked back towards Coppice Row. When we were a good twenty yards away, I sat down on a low wall and Wilson perched next to me.

"She might have been listening on the other side of the door," I explained. "No need to distress her – or alert her to our concerns."

Wilson nodded eagerly but said nothing.

"You can speak now," I said finally.

"Willoughby!" he blurted out. "John Willoughby – the man from Serle's."

"So..."

"So now we know the source of Willoughby's information – his own half-brother," said Wilson.

"A source which has now suddenly and completely dried up, as Thorpe is dead and we have the ledger."

"We know that," said Wilson slowly, "but does Willoughby?"

I paused. "He will soon know of his brother's death, as we will tell him. And he will know that it was murder. What he will not know is what has become of that book – whether it is safely hidden away by Thorpe, or whether it has been taken by his killer. That we might have it will probably not occur to him straight away, which buys us some time." Wilson was itching to be off, I could tell. "So what do you suggest we do next?"

"Tell Willoughby. Watch for a reaction," said Wilson.

"It will be controlled; this is a man who works as both poacher and gamekeeper, and he knows how to play his roles."

Wilson nodded curtly. "Then we follow him. His priority – once he has comforted his mother – will be to find out who knows what. Who killed his brother and why, and who has the book."

"And those he suspects are bound to be of interest to us as well."

CHAPTER TWENTY-SEVEN

Serious constable business

FRIDAY 16TH JUNE 1826 – AFTERNOON

John Willoughby may have been an accomplished player of parts, but his grief on hearing of the death of his brother was completely genuine. With his skin stretched thin over the sharp angles of his face, we could see the paleness of the shock and the reddening of his eyes all too clearly. In the small back office that we had been shown to after explaining the nature of our business, Willoughby clutched the seat of his chair.

"How?" he asked, his voice shaking with control or anger – I could not tell which.

Wilson glanced at me and I nodded. "He was taken from the street," Wilson said, "and bundled into an alley-way. There his throat was cut."

Willoughby closed his eyes momentarily, reminding me of how his mother had done the same.

"A robbery, do you think?" he asked.

"It would seem the most likely explanation," I agreed. "We understand that Mr Thorpe was..." I looked at Wilson as though uncertain.

He flipped open his notebook and said, "A jarvey". No need to let Willoughby think that we had more than a formal and passing interest in the sudden death of a man in our area of the metropolis.

"So he was unlikely to have had a great deal of money on him," I mused.

I watched Willoughby, and caught the most fleeting narrowing of his eyes as he saw an escape.

"Gil did mention a few nights ago that he had a regular who was very generous," he said, "so he might have been more flush in the pocket than usual. And of course, constables, we live in desperate times – poor wretches will cut an honest man's throat for the price of a size of ale."

"Indeed," I nodded regretfully. "It seems, as I say, the most likely explanation." Wilson made a show of closing his notebook and putting it into his pocket. We both stood, and Willoughby did the same. I shook his hand. "Our condolences once more, Mr Willoughby."

"Thank you," he said. "And it was good of you to come for my mother; she worries about me now almost as much as she did when I was a child."

I picked up my hat from the table. "I take it you will go to her now. This is hard news for a mother to sit with on her own."

"Of course – I just need to pass on some work to a fellow clerk and then I will go home."

Wilson and I had been waiting in a convenient doorway only a few minutes when Willoughby came out of the police office. He beckoned to one of the message lads loitering nearby and handed him a note before turning up towards Clerkenwell Road. The lad, meanwhile, started off in the other direction. Once Willoughby had turned the corner into Hatton Wall, we turned our step southwards. The message lad was now a little way ahead of us, but a sharp whistle and a cry of, "Lad – message!" soon brought him back.

"Constable Plank, sir!" he said. "I have an errand in hand," he held up the note for me to see, "but I can take yours too."

I was not surprised to be recognised; I had been using message lads since long before this one was born, and Martha's habit of feeding them meant that they squabbled over the privilege of patrolling near my house in order to get what they called 'a tip and a bite' for dealing with my messages.

I shook my head. "It's your errand that I'm interested in, my lad. May I see it?"

"Constable business, is it, sir? Or personal?"

I tried not to smile; the lads took pride in their work, and this one was wary of betraying a confidence. "I give you my word," I said solemnly, "that this is constable business – very serious constable business. To do with a brutal murder."

The lad's eyes widened. "The man in Peter Street this morning?" he asked in hushed tones. "The one with..." and he drew his finger across his throat.

I winked at him; it seemed safer than either lying or telling the truth. This satisfied him and he handed over the note. I unfolded it carefully – thankfully Willoughby had been in too much of a rush to seal it – and read these words: "My brother is killed. I know the location of the book and shall retrieve it. JW." There was no name on the outside of the note, but of course the lad would know the intended recipient. I handed back the re-folded note.

"Thank you – most helpful." I felt in my waistcoat pocket and pulled out a coin, which I passed over. The lad looked at it and smiled broadly. As he turned to go, I said, "By the by, lad – who are you delivering to?"

"One of yours, sir, at Great Marlborough Street – Mr Dawson."

"Mr Dawson?" asked Martha in amazement. "The magistrate who so dislikes you for favouring Mr Conant?" I nodded. "And what exactly did the note say?"

I took out my notebook and read the message aloud. She looked puzzled.

"But how can he know the location of the book?" she asked. "I can't imagine that Thorpe would have admitted to him that he left it behind in Mr Conant's rooms. What is clear is that he wants Mr Dawson to think that he – I mean Willoughby – knows where it is."

I nodded; she was right. "Maybe he suspects that Dawson had a hand in Thorpe's murder, and is making sure that he himself is safe – at least until the book is found."

"Could he, do you think – be involved in murder?" asked Martha.

"Mr Dawson?" I said. "Well, he is not a likeable fellow, that's true. He is short-tempered, and something of a bully, but more than that – murder? I do not like to think so."

"A constable cannot afford to dismiss things simply because he does not like to think them," said Martha gently.

CHAPTER TWENTY-EIGHT

Neither brains nor bravery

MONDAY 19TH JUNE 1826

I have rarely been as reluctant in my life as I was the following Monday. I arrived early at Great Marlborough Street, to see Mr Conant before he went into court for the day, and he was still eating breakfast when I knocked on his door. He indicated the pot on the sideboard, and I poured myself a cup of chocolate.

"Come, Sam, sit with me," he said, "and tell me what is troubling you." I must have looked surprised, because he added, "It is not only constables who learn to read faces, you know."

He then buttered a piece of toast and chewed it, making no further efforts to prod me into confession. I have long thought that this patience, this willingness to wait

215

until a man is ready to talk, is one of the characteristics that has made John Conant one of our fairest magistrates. And my admiration for him served on this day to make my reluctance even greater.

"Mr Conant," I said at last. He cocked an eyebrow at me and took another bite of toast. "Mr Conant," I started again, "you remember that we talked of Mr Percival of Hatton Garden."

"I do."

"And of the possibility that he might be acting in his own interests rather than those of his office." I chose my words as carefully as a young girl picking her way through a field of nettles.

"You have more information?" asked Conant.

I shook my head. "Well, maybe – more information, yes, but not concerning Mr Percival."

"I see." The magistrate swallowed the last of his toast, wiped his mouth and fingers with his napkin, dropped it onto his plate and pushed both away from him. He sat back in his chair, laced his hands in his lap, and waited. I knew this habit too: if you interrupt and suggest words, a man will leap on them and use them. But wait for him to supply his own, and he will inevitably paint a more truthful picture.

I took a deep breath; there was now no going back. I told him of our discovery of the connection between

Thorpe and Willoughby, and of Willoughby's actions after hearing of his brother's death.

"I was not surprised when he sent a note to warn his fellow conspirators," I said, "but I was surprised to see to whom he sent it." I swallowed. "It was addressed to Mr Dawson – here." I pointed downwards to indicate the courthouse below us.

It was my turn to watch Conant's face for a reaction, and I saw only resignation – not disgust or horror, and certainly not surprise.

"Ah," said the magistrate. "Mr Dawson."

I nodded.

"And what exactly do you think is Mr Dawson's role in all of this?"

"I have been pondering this since Friday, sir, and I think I may have an idea. Any criminal crew that has the co-operation of a magistrate is guaranteed certain protection – from interference, and, should it come to it, from conviction. With two magistrates, the load can be shared – and with them working in different courts, the hope must be that no-one would connect the actions of the two."

Conant stood and went to look out of the window; I wondered if he knew that he did this whenever he was thinking deeply about something.

He spoke with his back to me. "Dawson cannot be the leader. He does not have the brains, or the bravery." He looked over his shoulder. "Although we could not use that opinion as evidence, of course. However widely it might be shared."

"I agree, sir," I said. "I was of the same view. I should imagine that Mr Dawson's services have been secured in the same way as those of the doctor – with offers of payment in kind."

The magistrate returned to his chair, shaking his head. "I doubt that such offers would be of much interest to Mr Dawson. His preferences lie... elsewhere." He gave me a level look.

"Given what we know of this conspiracy," I replied, "that would work just as well for their purposes, especially when coupled with the threat of exposure. As you may remember, Thorpe admitted – or at least did not deny – that they accuse men of sodomitical assaults in order to secure payments. Perhaps in Mr Dawson's case, they are seeking not money, but assistance."

"At least there would be some truth in the levelling of such accusations against him," said Conant, then looked at me sharply. He knew as well as I that such whispers could end a career.

"Perhaps it would be wise to concentrate on the aspects of Mr Dawson's behaviour that are more closely connected with his magisterial duties," I suggested.

"Indeed," said Conant, nodding. "What do you propose?"

"So far, all we have is that note from Willoughby. Mr Dawson could easily claim that it was misaddressed, or that Willoughby – in desperation – was simply trying to deflect attention and blame onto anyone else who came to mind. What we need, before you can go to the Lord Chancellor with your concerns, is examples of occasions on which Mr Dawson has abused his office." I felt myself frown as a vague memory returned to me.

"What is it, Sam?" asked the magistrate, as vigilant as ever.

"It may be nothing," I said, "but some weeks ago I saw three men being taken into court, here. They were charged with disorderly conduct – arrested by Constable Wayman on your warrant. All acquitted by Mr Dawson."

"Wrongly, in your opinion?"

I held up my hands. "It is not for me to say, sir: I thank my stars daily that I am not called upon to judge men, only to arrest them."

Conant rolled his eyes. "I mean, Sam," he said carefully, "in your view, did these men look as though they were capable of disorderly conduct?"

"Aye. Two of them I knew of old, and disorderly was their regular state. And that morning, they were certainly clipping the King's English."

"So you were surprised when they were acquitted?"

"Yes, I was, but Bert – Constable Wayman – was not. He called them," I flipped back in my notebook, "'Mr Dawson's special verdicts'."

"What I don't understand," said Martha as she held a needle up to the light of the window and tried to thread it, "is why this Mr Dawson made such a fuss about you not working for him. Surely, if he is in league with Willoughby and the others, the last thing he will want is you sniffing around. After all," she smiled with satisfaction as the cotton finally slipped through the eye of the needle, "he can be in no doubt about your honesty."

"But maybe that is the very thing he counts on," I suggested. "If he passes some of his business through me, it makes the rest of it look more respectable by association."

"And I daresay that by favouring Mr Conant over him, you have made him a little jealous," she said.

"I'm not sure that jealous is quite the right word," I replied. "But perhaps he does feel slighted, as though I am indicating by my actions that Mr Conant's warrants are more worthy of my time than his."

"And those whose reputations are the most precarious will often defend them more fiercely."

"The lady doth protest too much, you mean?"

Martha finished her stitching and bit off the thread. "Or the magistrate, in this case. It seems to me that you will have to swallow your distaste and spend a little more time with Mr Dawson."

CHAPTER TWENTY-NINE

The under-footman

MONDAY 26TH JUNE 1826

And so it was that I deliberately made myself available to Mr Dawson. I was careful not to alter my behaviour too dramatically, and I pretended reluctance when the mood took me. Mr Conant played his part by claiming that the heat had diminished his own appetite for work – it was certainly sweltering. I also mentioned in one or two ears – ears that I trusted not to keep a secret – that I was entrusting Wilson with more responsibility, and he was happy to strut about the place without me. If I was honest with myself, he was more than ready to work alone on simpler warrants, but I hoped selfishly that he would not enjoy his independence too much.

For a few days all was well: warrants were issued, arrests were made, verdicts were found and punishments were given. Although it was clear that Mr Dawson ran his court in a very different manner to Mr Conant – less listening and more bluster would be a kind way to put it – there was nothing that made me especially uneasy.

On Monday morning, Tom Neale and I were sitting in the front office, waiting for Mr Dawson to finish his morning's hearings and discussing the violent storm of the previous evening – incessant lightning for three hours – when the door was barged open and in came a young lad half-dragging, half-carrying a sobbing girl. Her clothes were fine enough, but her skirt was brown with mud and there was a rip to her chemise. Her hair had come unpinned on one side, and it gave her a pitiful lop-sided look like a puppet with a broken string. Tom took one look at them and said, "Back office. Tea."

Taking an arm each, the lad and I led the girl down the corridor and into the small room, guiding her to a chair. She fell into it, still crying, and leaned onto the table with renewed sobs. The lad looked at me helplessly. I pointed to another chair.

"Sit," I said, "and stay." He did so.

A minute later, there was a light knock at the door and Tom appeared with a tray. "I've added a slice of seed cake each – she certainly looks in need of it."

At the suggestion of food, our lady visitor lifted her head from the table. From the paint on her face, I could make a guess at her profession.

"Could you fetch a damp cloth, please, Mr Neale," I said. "I think this young lady might need a little tidying."

Tom took a quick look at her, saw what I had seen, and went for the cloth. When he returned, he handed it to her and she wordlessly wiped at her skin and handed the soiled cloth back to him. Tom looked at it ruefully – it would take some cleaning. Once the red and black had been removed, the clear face of a child looked back at me. About the age of Alice, I thought.

I caught the lad staring at her; no doubt he had been fooled into thinking her a grown woman.

"Yours?" I asked.

He shook his head, and his shocked paleness confirmed it.

"I... I was in the yard, filling the coal scuttles."

"Where?" I asked.

"New Burlington Street – I'm under-footman at number twelve. Hopkins. George Hopkins." And indeed he was in the plain dark breeches, waistcoat and coat that those of his profession wore for morning duties. "I heard a cry – a woman's cry – and then a thud, and when I looked out into the street, I saw her." He indicated the girl with his head. "She was lying in the street, crying. I went to help her – I couldn't very well take her into the house, not a woman like that..." He blushed slightly as he realised what he had said, but she appeared not to take offence. "And so I brought her here."

"Do you help every woman you see lying in the street?" I asked. He shook his head. "Then why this one?"

"She seemed... in a bad way," he muttered. "After the cry, I heard a carriage rolling away. At that time of the morning we have carts making deliveries, but not many carriages. When I went to help her, I looked round and saw the carriage turning out into Regent Street, and I thought I recognised it."

I looked across at the girl; without her paint, she looked very young, and very pale.

"Were you taken there in a carriage?" I asked.

She bit her lip and said nothing. Her eyes kept straying to the cake on the tray. "Help yourself," I said, and her little hand darted out and daintily broke off a corner which she nibbled. When she thought no-one was looking, she went back for more.

"So you think she was thrown out of the carriage?" I asked Hopkins.

He nodded. "But that's not it," he said. "That's not what worried me." He shifted in his seat to check that the girl was still distracted by her food, then beckoned me closer. I leaned towards him. "Her skirt," he whispered. "That's not just mud on it. When I found her, she was not, well, not completely covered. And it was all down her legs. It's blood."

And on cue, there was a gentle sigh as the girl slid from the chair to the floor.

Doctor Weston came quickly from his surgery in Silver Street; his puffing as he came into the back office confirmed that the message lad had passed on my sense of urgency. Hopkins and I had lifted the girl onto the table, and Tom had rolled up one blanket to put under her head and laid a second one over her. The doctor waved us all out of the room and pushed the door closed. By now Hopkins was nearly as pale as his charge, and he and I sat together on a bench in the corridor.

After a few minutes the door opened and the doctor came out, turning down his cuffs and buttoning them. He beckoned us along the corridor into the front office before he spoke.

"You were right to call me," he said, giving the young footman a look of approval. "She is young and therefore strong, but her injuries are serious." He shook his head. The surgeon and I were perhaps more worldly than the footman, who looked puzzled.

"Her injuries, are they internal, doctor?" I asked.

He nodded. "She has recently had intimate relations with a man – perhaps more than one man – and they have been... unkind in their attentions. Very unkind. She has lost a great deal of blood, and may be damaged. And she has recently had a child and has yet to heal from that."

The footman looked horrified. "But she's only a child – without all that muck on her face, anyone can see she's no more than fourteen." He looked down the corridor towards the back office. "I have a sister that age. And the thought..."

I grasped his shoulder. "Then do not think it. We all have to learn not to think certain things, otherwise we should go mad. You have done a brave and compassionate thing, bringing her to us. Doctor Weston will know best how to care for her."

I looked at the surgeon and he nodded. "I will take her to the Magdalen Hospital in St George's Fields," he said. "They rescue fallen women," he held up a hand as Hopkins opened his mouth to object, "but also victims of seduction, and they are particularly skilled at caring for younger women. I will sponsor her application, and I feel confident they will admit her." He smiled kindly at the footman, who smiled thinly in return. "Tom, will you arrange a coach for me and the young lady – south of the river." The office keeper nodded and the doctor returned to his patient.

Hopkins turned to leave.

"Before you go, Mr Hopkins," I said, "we will need to have a little word about precisely what you saw." He glanced up at the clock on the wall behind the office keeper's counter. "I know you will be missed, but we have already sent word to New Burlington Street that you went to the gallant assistance of a lady in distress. A few minutes more, and then you can head off with a note from me for your butler, more fully explaining – excusing – your absence from morning duties."

Tom knocked on the door to say that a coach had been brought round, and the doctor came out, the blanket-draped girl still senseless in his arms, and edged his way along the corridor.

"My bag, if you would, constable," he said as he passed us pressed against the wall. I retrieved it for him, and followed them out to the coach. I climbed in first, putting his bag on the floor, and Doctor Weston handed the girl in to me; she weighed so little. I settled her on the cushions inside, tucking the blanket around her, before descending so that the doctor could take my place. I closed the door and then called up to the jarvey, "The Magdalen Hospital – as gently as you can." He nodded, flicked his whip, and the coach pulled away.

In the back office, I once again sat down with George Hopkins and took out my notebook.

"How long have you worked in your current position?" I asked.

"Just under three years – I started there when I was fourteen," he replied.

"And do you enjoy your work?"

He looked surprised at the question but answered readily enough. "It is a respectable household. The butler is a taskmaster, but fair. And the grub is good."

"Always important, that," I said, smiling. "I ask because sometimes people say things that are not quite true in order to make trouble for others, or to escape a situation that does not please them."

He shook his head vehemently. "Oh no, sir – not at all." I believed him.

"Well, then, to this morning. You said that you were filling the coal scuttles in the yard, when you heard a woman's cry and then a thud." He nodded. "Which was probably our young lady being pushed or thrown out of a carriage." He nodded again. "Because you heard a carriage driving away."

"Yes, and I saw it too – only the back half of it, as it was turning into Regent Street."

"Heading north or south?" I asked.

He paused in recollection. "North – up towards Oxford Circus." I made a note.

"And what did this carriage look like?"

"It was a landau," he said promptly, "drawn by a pair, from the sound of it."

"The top – open or closed?"

"Closed – at least, the back half, and it would be unusual to close the back and leave the front open." Martha would laugh when I told her of this conversation; she often observed that all young men were obsessed with carriages and coaches, the faster and fancier the better.

"And you said that you thought you recognised the carriage."

Hopkins nodded. "The colours were familiar – very distinctive. A dark green body with yellow door panels and accents, and yellow on the wheels."

"Very fancy," I said. "And you've seen these colours before?"

"A few weeks ago we had a grand party to celebrate the young master's coming of age. One of the guests arrived in a phaeton in that livery. Alexander Yates-Drummond." He looked at me. "Eldest son of Adolphus Yates-Drummond."

"Member of Parliament," I finished.

"And what do you know of this Yates-Drummond MP?" asked Martha as she rinsed a plate and handed it to me for drying.

"Very little this morning, but I have asked around and he seems a solid sort: Tory, estate in Cheshire, family money going back centuries, married to the daughter of a baronet. No scandal about the father, but the heir apparent – Alexander – is a rackety sort by all accounts."

"Too much money and not enough occupation?" asked Martha, shaking her hands and wiping them on her apron.

I nodded. "He may be in line to inherit everything material, but the family brains have definitely not found their way to young Alexander, according to Lily."

Martha smiled as she took the last dish from me and stacked it in the cupboard. "As if I need to ask your source of society information."

"She called in to see her father this afternoon, and I just happened to mention the name to her," I said with pretend outrage; my wife liked to tease me about my fondness for Conant's daughter. "Not at all her sort of fellow, she said; too used to getting his own way."

"Well, that would certainly cause sparks," said Martha, "given that Miss Lily is quite fond of her own way too."

We moved through into the sitting room and Martha picked up the book that was waiting for us on the little table by her chair. We were a few chapters into "Northanger Abbey", which Lily herself had recommended, and I must confess that I was enjoying it more than I had imagined I would. I usually prefer more action and adventure, but Miss Austen's sharp observations and economical turn of phrase made me think that she would have made an admirable constable.

Martha had read only a few sentences when there was a knock at the back door – a message lad, then, or perhaps

Wilson. Martha paused with her finger marking her place in the text, and I went to see who it was.

"If it's a lad," Martha called after me, "there's plums in the bowl – give him one." No wonder we never had trouble finding someone to run our errands. And indeed it was a lad – one of the younger ones, left on duty while the older ones had their supper. I handed over a coin and a plum and then, seeing his large hungry eyes, another plum. He grinned and ran off.

"It's from Doctor Weston," I said, unfolding the note. A very fine chain, broken, with a tiny crucifix on it fell into my hand. "Probably news about that girl." I scanned the few words.

Martha leaned forward and touched my knee. "What is it, Sam? You look quite pale all of a sudden."

I handed her the note. "She died, Martha. In the coach, before they even reached the Magdalen. Loss of blood, Weston says."

"Oh, Sam." My wife knelt in front of me and looked up at me, her face pale and her eyes brimming with tears. "How shameful."

"That's the word alright, Martha – that's the very word. It is shameful. It's a shame on all of us, that a young girl can be picked up, abused and damaged like that, and then just thrown away to die."

Martha nodded. "And the poor child had a baby, it seems: the note says that she gave that crucifix to the doctor to pass on to her baby." Martha held out her hand and I passed over the pitiful item. She looked at it and then gasped. "Dear God, Sam – I've seen this before. That night at the Blue Boar. See," she leaned forward and pointed at the back of the tiny cross, "there's an E scratched into the back of it." She looked at me with tears in her eyes. "I think that poor girl might have been Alice's friend Ellen."

I have rarely seen Martha as angry as she was that night. And much of her anger was directed at me. When people pretend anger, they wave their arms and shout, but real anger – white-hot, controlled anger – is an altogether more frightening sight.

"Bait," spat Martha with bitterness as she stood over me. "That's how you saw them, those poor wretches in Harrison Street." I stood and reached for her, but she snatched her arm away from me. "After you went to see Mr Freame and told him what his charitable funds were being used for, you could have closed the place down. I told you to rescue them, but your precious enquiries always come first. And where have they got you now? What have your enquiries revealed so far?" I went to speak, but she held up her hand. "I'll tell you: two dead bodies, and you and Mr Conant still reluctant to upset the applecart."

And as we lay in bed that night, each silent and isolated, I cursed myself. God forgive me, had I lost sight of the true victims at the heart of all the scheming and cleverness?

CHAPTER THIRTY

Burlington Arcade

TUESDAY 27TH JUNE 1826 – MORNING

As Mr Dawson – unlike Mr Conant – did not have rooms in Great Marlborough Street, I had to wait until he arrived to prepare for the day's hearings before I could apply for my warrant. He installed himself at the bench, glanced cursorily at the pile of papers that the clerk had assembled for him, and then proceeded to dig around in his teeth with an ivory toothpick. I stood in the well of the courtroom, willing myself to look outwardly patient: I would not give him the satisfaction of knowing that I was irritated by his behaviour. At last he took the pick from his mouth, peered at it, wiped it on his gown, and tucked it away in his waistcoat pocket.

"Constable Plank," he said flatly.

The clerk readied himself at his record book to take a note of my application.

"A serious assault, sir, yesterday, after which the victim – a young girl – has died."

Dawson scratched his neck under his collar, setting his jowls wobbling. He looked supremely unconcerned.

"There was a witness," I added.

"To the act?" he yawned.

I shook my head. "To the aftermath. He found the girl and brought her to us. She had been violated."

"A drab, then," he sniffed. Dawson had certainly been at the back of the queue when compassion was handed out.

I held my temper. "Whatever her reason for being where she was, the fact remains that she has died thanks to the actions of another. Murder, sir. Or manslaughter, at the very least."

"So all you need, constable, is for me to hear the bare facts and then send it to a superior tribunal for their careful attention." He looked down at the clerk who nodded in agreement. "Very well, proceed – but make haste, as I need to use the pot before the first hearing."

I laid before him the facts of the situation, starting with the arrival of Hopkins and ending with the death of the girl.

"And you say that this... under-footman thought he recognised the carriage."

"He seemed quite certain, sir – he had seen the livery before."

"So it is someone from the family that owns this carriage who will be called?" I nodded. "Very well." He snapped his fingers at the clerk, who leapt out of his seat and handed a warrant to Dawson. The magistrate dipped his pen and looked at me. "The name, constable?"

"Yates-Drummond, sir," I said. "Alexander Yates-Drummond."

Dawson blinked rapidly. His jaw tightened, and he laid down his pen with exaggerated care. The clerk scurried back to his stool and started sorting papers.

"Constable Plank," said the magistrate slowly and with great care, as though speaking to an imbecile, "did it not occur to you to mention that you were levelling accusations against one of our most important families? You are aware that Mr Adolphus Yates-Drummond is a Member of Parliament?"

"No, sir, it did not, and yes, sir, I am," I said. The clerk, if it were possible, bent even lower over his papers. "The crime concerns me; the status of those involved does not."

"I see," said Dawson. "It is as well, then, constable," and he laid heavy emphasis on the word, "that this is my decision and not yours." He slipped the incomplete warrant under a ledger and stood. The clerk scrambled to his feet. And with a dismissive wave of his hand the magistrate swept from the courtroom, no doubt in search of the pot.

By good fortune the first person I saw on leaving the courtroom was Wilson. He was sitting on the bench in the front office, spitting on a cloth and buffing the toes of his boots. He looked up at me with concern.

"Are you well, sir? You look very flushed."

"I'm furious, Wilson, so furious I can hardly see straight." I bit off the words. "That... that fool in there," I waved my arm in the direction of the courtroom.

Tom Neale appeared behind the counter. "Best get him out of here for a while, Will," he said. "Let him simmer down. Here: take this one – it's just what he needs today." He handed Wilson a scrap of paper. "Complaint from a beadle in the arcade – pickpockets again."

I'll say this for Wilson: he knows when to keep quiet. We strode down the steps and turned towards Regent Street, where we headed south and then right into New Burlington Street. I did not expect to find anything; I simply wanted to see where it had all happened, where a young girl had been thrown away like yesterday's peelings. All was quiet; we were too late for deliveries and too early for social calls, and the only person we saw was a nursemaid wheeling her charge in a perambulator, probably heading for the shady relief of the gardens in Golden Square. Wilson touched his hat and she smiled shyly. We continued down Savile Street then into Vigo Lane, and entered Burlington Arcade from the north.

Once, not long after it had opened, I had brought Martha here to gaze into the windows. I remember that she was torn between disdain for the ridiculous fripperies on offer at such inflated prices, and longing for some of the items she saw. Indeed, the displays in the windows were so beguiling – so ever-changing and gorgeous – that pickpockets quickly learnt that passers-by would be reliably distracted and absorbed. In consequence, customers were complaining to shopkeepers that they would avoid the area if measures were not taken to protect them. But pickpockets are among the slipperiest of criminals, and even the resident beadles did not deter them.

One of these beadles, sweating majestically in his splendid top hat and frock coat, was approaching us now. Wilson showed him the slip of paper, and he pointed down the arcade.

"Madame Fontaine – glove maker – halfway down on the right," he said.

"French?" asked Wilson.

"About as French as I am," replied the beadle with a wink, "but she swears it sells more gloves."

When we tried the door of Madame Fontaine's shop – "Purveyor of fine Continental ladies' gloves and hosiery" was engraved on the fanlight – it was locked. Wilson rapped on the glass, and a woman's head appeared above the counter. Her cap was awry and one of her curls had come unpinned and was dangling over her cheek. She looked about fifty, and was pink with exertion.

"Constables, madam," called Wilson. "From Great Marlborough Street."

She nodded vigorously. "I have him!" she called back with some satisfaction, and in an accent that was definitely more Piccadilly than Paris. "I have him here!"

There were then some sounds of struggle and scuffle, the head disappeared, and a small grubby hand appeared momentarily on the floor alongside the counter before being dragged back again. Wilson and I looked at each other.

"Are you sitting on him, Madame Fontaine?" I shouted through the door.

"That I am, constable, and he's going nowhere!" Her head appeared once more, a triumphant look in evidence.

I glanced up the arcade towards the beadle, who raised his eyebrows at me and then ostentatiously turned his back and continued his patrol away from us.

"Madame Fontaine," I called with some exasperation, "we cannot continue like this. We need to arrest this person, which we cannot do while you and he remain locked in your shop and we are outside. Do you see that?"

She nodded, and rose slightly as though riding a bucking horse, presumably as the pickpocket made another attempt to escape.

"You see that I have with me a very large constable." I indicated Wilson. "He is about the size of your doorway."

She took a moment to assess the relative dimensions and then nodded.

"If you will release your captive and unlock the door, I guarantee that he will not manage to squeeze past Constable Wilson."

Madame Fontaine cocked her head to one side, and then pulled herself to her feet, walked around the counter and came to the door. A lad of no more than eight crawled out from behind the counter and looked up at me.

"And you," I said loudly, pointing at him, "stay there. Otherwise Constable Wilson will sit on you instead, and that you may not survive."

Once the door was unlocked Wilson and I entered the little shop, with Wilson immediately taking up his familiar position with his back to the door. Since Thorpe had given him the slip back at Great Marlborough Street, I knew he would take no chances.

"Stand up, lad," I said to the boy on the floor. He picked himself up, dusted down his trousers – an action which made little difference as they were filthy anyway – and stood in front of me with his head bowed.

"That's him," said the proprietress with satisfaction. "Caught him at it myself. Digging his grubby little paw into the pocket of a fine gentleman, right outside my window here. The gentleman and I pushed him into the shop, and I locked him in with me. The gentleman said he would ask the beadle to summon you."

I took out my notebook. "And this gentleman's name?" I asked.

"Well, now," said Madame Fontaine coyly. "He would prefer that I not divulge." She gave me a heavy wink. "He was choosing something for a lady friend."

"The paramours of your customers are of no interest to me, Mrs Fontaine," I said.

"Madame," she corrected. "Madame Josephine Fontaine." She indicated the lettering on the window.

I ignored her. "Without the name of the alleged victim, it will be hard for us to prosecute."

The smile left her face. "We both know that that is not true, don't we, constable. This... this creature is a reputed thief, and it is entirely within your powers – your duties, constable – to take him before the court." She folded her arms with righteousness.

"I see you know the law of England, Madame Fontaine – no doubt you studied it on your journey here from Paris." She narrowed her eyes at me but said nothing. I continued. "Am I to understand that you wish me to arrest this child – this starving child – and see him committed to a house of correction for six months' hard labour?"

"I do," she said firmly. The boy twisted his hands in anguish.

"You believe then, Madame Fontaine, that the laws should be applied absolutely, without mercy?"

The woman was too foolish to recognise a trap when it was set. She nodded emphatically, and her silly bonnet bobbed. "I do indeed, constable," she said.

"In that case, Constable Wilson, when we have finished with this little rogue, I would like you to check the rooms above," I pointed at the ceiling with my pencil, "to make sure that they are not being let out for immoral purposes. You cannot be too careful, Madame Fontaine," I said to the woman who was now clutching at her lace fichu with a trembling hand. "The upper storeys of several premises in the arcade have been used by ladies of ill repute..."

The woman licked her lips nervously as she considered her dilemma. She reached a decision. "I can assure you, constables, that my rooms above are used purely for storage. There is a bed in one, to be sure, but that is for me; sometimes a late order or early delivery means that I need to remain on the premises. There is no need for you to trouble yourselves by checking. And if you are satisfied that this poor child can be dealt with in another manner, then," she smiled sweetly, "I am more than happy to leave it to your discretion. Your discretion, constables, is what I count on."

The three of us walked back up Cork Street. Just for show, in case his gang-leader was watching, Wilson and I each held one of the lad's arms, but all the fight had long since gone out of him.

"Back to the police office?" asked Wilson. The boy looked up at me. I nodded.

"But no need to worry, lad," I said. "Constable Wilson and I have a plan." We turned the corner. "And it's a good one, so if we let go of you, will you promise not to make a run for it?" The lad looked uncertain.

"Otherwise," said Wilson, "you'll miss out on the best roast pork roll in all of London. We usually get one this time of day, and if you come with us, well, I daresay we could stretch to a third."

I could hear the boy swallowing; he all but drooled at the thought. The deal struck, we took a detour to visit Wakefields and Wilson bought a roll stuffed with roast pork for our little captive. While Wilson was distracted by his own food, I slipped a few coins into his pocket;

with a widowed mother and several little ones at home, he could ill afford to feed another mouth.

Suitably cooled by a tumbler each of lemonade, we made our way back to Great Marlborough Street. As he looked up the steps leading to the front office the lad – he had by now vouchsafed that his name was Joseph – hesitated. I put a hand on his shoulder and we walked up them together.

Tom looked over the counter at Joseph.

"Mr Neale," I said, "this is Joseph." The keeper held out his hand and the lad shook it. "He is fed and watered, and now in need of good and legal employment. Did I hear Jem Butler saying the other day that the owner of his coach was looking for a stable boy?"

Joseph looked up at me with shining eyes. "Horses?" he asked.

I nodded. "Big beasts. Not fond of them myself. You?"

"I think they're magnificent," he breathed.

"Magnificent, heh?" laughed Tom. "Someone's been eavesdropping on the fine folk in the arcade, picking up words like that. Come with me, Joseph, and I'll get one of the jarveys to take you round to the coachyard, with Constable Plank's recommendation."

I nodded. "Thank you, Tom. And you were right: that was just what I needed."

"You and Mrs Plank," said Tom with a smile. "You won't be happy until you've found a place for every waif and stray in London." The mention of Martha reminded me that I had no intention of going home without some progress to report to her.

CHAPTER THIRTY-ONE

A great deal of prattle

TUESDAY 27TH JUNE 1826 – AFTERNOON

As Wilson and I waved the coach off down the street, with Joseph sitting up by the jarvey and looking as proud as Punch, I heard the noon bell being rung at the workhouse. Dawson would be rising from the bench; he was not one to let unfinished business delay his meal. I gave it five minutes and then went into the courtroom. As I had hoped, the clerk was there alone, writing in his court record book.

"Mr Jamison," I said. The clerk looked up at me. "Mr Jamison, I wish to enquire about the matter I brought before Mr Dawson this morning." The clerk looked, if possible, even more nervous, and glanced around the courtroom as though searching for spies. He closed the record book.

"This morning?" he said hesitantly.

I nodded. "The young lady and the under-footman, the carriage – you remember. Murder or manslaughter."

Jamison placed his hand on top of the book. "I remember nothing..." he cleared his throat, "nothing of that, constable."

I was astonished. "Mr Jamison," I said more loudly than I had intended, and the miserable man shuddered. I moderated my tone. "Mr Jamison, are you telling me that you have no recollection of a discussion that Mr Dawson and I had in this very room not three hours since?" He said nothing. "You half-completed a warrant and passed it up to the bench. Mr Dawson put it under a ledger." I looked up at the bench, but the pile of books – including the ledger and presumably the warrant – had disappeared. "You made notes in your book – I saw you."

I walked across to the clerk's desk, and Jamison picked up his record book and held it to him, as a child clutches a much-loved toy. I looked at him.

After a minute of terrible silence, he spoke in a low voice, trembling all the while. "Constable Plank," he said, "I am a lowly second clerk. I have an elderly father and an invalid spinster sister at home; they rely on me for everything. I need this position." He shut his eyes and swallowed hard. "Mr Dawson is a demanding man, constable

– and a powerful one. A word from him, and I would be dismissed. Please understand that I must do all I can to prevent him saying that word."

The clerk unfolded his arms and gently placed the record book on the table. I pulled it towards me and leafed through it until I reached the page with today's date at the top, neatly underlined, followed by a list of the morning's business: an application for a licence for a public house, two bakers reported for short weight, a disorderly apprentice – on it went, but no mention of my case. Remembering something my banker friend Freame had once said to me about studying ledgers, I ran my finger down the centre of the book, and it was unmistakable: a page had been torn out.

Jamison hung his head. "I must do all I can, constable."

I waited as long as I could that evening, having sent word to Martha that I would be late home – although I was not sure that the news would distress her much, given her current view of me. One by one the constables and clerks left, then Tom, and eventually even George Cooper, the gaoler.

"Make sure to lock up behind you, Sam," he said as he shrugged on his coat. "I don't know what it is about a police office, but those on the inside always want to get out, and those on the outside always want to get in."

I jangled my keys at him. "No need to worry, George. I'll leave the place as tight as a dandy's inexpressibles."

"Ha!" he said. "Give me a comfortable pair of cossacks any day."

I was dozing on the bench in the front office when Mr Conant's footman Williams – or Thin Billy as we in the police office called him, thanks to his spare frame – shook me by the shoulder.

"Mr Conant is back now, sir, and says you're to come up."

I stood, rubbed my face to wake myself, checked my watch and saw that it had just gone two. I straightened my clothes and followed Thin Billy out of the main door. I stopped and locked it behind me, taking care to try it twice to make certain.

"Strict instructions from Mr Cooper?" asked the footman with a smile. I nodded, and followed him up the stairs to the magistrate's dining room.

"That will do, thank you, Williams," said Conant as we walked in. "You may go to bed – Constable Plank will see himself out."

The footman walked to the sideboard and laid his hand on the coffee pot to check that it was still warm, and then left. Mr Conant poured himself a cup and raised his eyebrow at me. I nodded and he poured a second cup and passed it to me. He sat in one of the armchairs and I took the other. He was in undress, his coat and cravat discarded.

"That was a truly ghastly evening," he said after a reviving sip of coffee. "The things we do for information, eh, Sam? It's bad enough occasionally sharing a bench with that old windbag, but having to dine with him as well was just... ghastly."

"Did Mr Dawson think it odd that you should invite him to your club?"

"Brooks's is not the natural home for such a cradle Tory as our good friend, but if someone else is paying the bill, he will dine anywhere. And dine he did. Course after course. He's well on his way to a cart load." Conant shook his head in wonder.

"Were you able to discuss the matter with him, sir?" I asked.

Conant stretched his legs out and sighed. "I was, constable, yes – although I had to suffer through a great deal of prattle to get there."

I could see the magistrate's eyes beginning to close; no doubt he had had to take a cup or two alongside Dawson to keep him company.

"The Yates-Drummond case, sir," I prompted. "Did you ask him about it?"

Conant blinked exaggeratedly at me and nodded slowly. "I did, Sam, yes, I did. And Mr Dawson is of the view that it is a family matter. He has already spoken to the father, and the honourable member has assured Mr Dawson that his son will be dealt with appropriately. It's all a question of names, said Mr Dawson: the son has a fine one and the girl had none, so why make a fuss?"

The magistrate's chin dropped onto his chest. I stood and gently took the cup from his hand, placing it on the table, and then lifted his feet onto a low stool and slipped off his shoes. Finally, I retrieved his coat from its hook and laid it over him before extinguishing the lights, shutting the door quietly and walking carefully down the stairs.

CHAPTER THIRTY-TWO

Suffer the innocents

WEDNESDAY 28TH JUNE 1826

After a few hours of restless sleep and an all but wordless breakfast, I put on my coat. This time I wanted Mrs Marwood to know exactly who I was. I had left a note at Great Marlborough Street for Tom Neale, asking him to send Wilson off on some sort of errand to keep him occupied for the morning. I wanted no help – and no witness.

It was a long and muggy walk, but the discomfort suited my mood – if anything, it worsened my temper. The new gardens in Tavistock Square were taking shape, and ordinarily I would have taken note of the changes to report back to Martha, but today I simply strode past. On Sidmouth Street I paused at a horse-trough to rinse my hands and splash my face, and then I turned towards the lodging house. I banged on the door and, as on my first visit back in April, I heard heavy footsteps before the door was opened by an unsmiling maid – Matthews, I recalled. I met her scowl for scowl.

"I am Constable Samuel Plank of Great Marlborough Street," I said. "I am here to see Mrs Marwood. I shall wait for her in the parlour."

The maid tried to shut the door in my face, but I pushed it open again. "Find your mistress – now."

Just then we both heard a noise from the kitchen downstairs. Matthews looked at me and seemed to come to a decision. "There's a back way out into the alley – round the corner," she said, pointing.

"You wait here, or it will be the worse for you," I said, and ran into Frances Street just as Mrs Marwood emerged from the alley that the maid had described.

"If you wish, Mrs Marwood," I called to her, "I can raise the hue and cry and summon all of your neighbours to my aid, or you can return quietly with me to your parlour."

She hesitated for a moment, and then glanced down – in her house slippers and apron, she was unlikely to outrun anyone. She tossed her head in defiance and walked towards me. I took her arm, none too gently I will admit, and steered her back through her own front door. Matthews, as instructed, was waiting.

The parlour was as I remembered, although today one set of curtains was drawn against the fierce sun. I took the two upright chairs and placed them in the middle of the room, facing each other. I pointed at one. "Sit," I said to Marwood, and she did so. I sat in the other.

"I know you now," she said, peering at me. Poor eyesight, as evidenced by the lorgnette on a ribbon around her neck. "You came here two or three months ago, asking about Alice Godfrey."

I nodded. "Alice, you will be pleased to know, is thriving and happy – and well beyond your clutches."

"All of my girls..." she began indignantly.

I stood and looked down at her. "Don't you dare," I said with a tremor in my voice as I tried to control it, "don't you dare pretend that you have even the slightest concern for the poor creatures you keep under your disgusting and sinful roof."

Marwood pressed her lips together and folded her hands primly in her lap.

I sat down again. "I am here today about another girl – Ellen. Don't waste my time by pretending not to know her. Ellen was in your care," I put as much venom as I could muster into the words, "when she fell pregnant. She overheard the agonies of another girl dying in childbirth, and she saw Doctor Fuller removing the bodies." I could tell from the widening of Marwood's eyes that she was alarmed by how much I knew. "This terrified her and Ellen ran away. The kind people who had taken Alice into their home agreed to shelter Ellen as well. Two weeks later, Ellen was thrown from a carriage, and died." The news was no surprise to Marwood, so doubtless someone had alerted her – there were eyes everywhere in London. "And you are going to tell me what happened in those two weeks. Aren't you, Matthews?"

I turned to look over my shoulder. The maid was standing where we had left her in the hallway, and I beckoned her into the parlour. She came reluctantly, twisting her apron in her hands.

"Your mistress, Matthews, knows the way of these things. She is working for a vile crew, and at this very moment is trying to work out whom she should fear more: them or me. I can assure you that it is me. And you have a similar decision to make. The outlook is bleak for your mistress, and you know as well as I that she will spare little thought for you as she tries to save her own skin. On the other hand, those who are helpful to constables often find that a kindly word about them is dropped in the ear of the judge." At the mention of a judge, Matthews put a grimy hand to her mouth and whimpered. "So tell me, Matthews, what happened after Ellen ran away?"

The maid moved very slightly closer to me, as I had known she would.

"She came back," she said quietly. "She had her baby at that coaching inn, like you said, the one where Alice lives. But they had no room for her and she had to leave."

"Surely they didn't just throw her out?" I asked – I couldn't believe that of Mr and Mrs Atkins.

"She told them she had somewhere to go – she didn't want them to worry. She slept out a couple of nights, she told me, but she was scared for the baby, and she came back here. The mistress said she could have her old place, but only if she earned it. So she went back to work."

"And the baby?" I asked. "Ellen's baby?"

Matthews sniffed loudly. "She left him here when she was out. I'd keep an eye on him, or one of the other girls – he was no trouble, the little mite. And then when Ellen didn't come back, the mistress said she knew someone who would take care of him – someone who liked babies. And when she took him yesterday afternoon, I followed her."

"Why?" I asked.

By now the maid was crying freely. "I wanted to see where she took him. She said the same to me, last December, when I had my baby – that she knew someone who would take care of her. My little girl. Flora, I called her. Dark curly hair, she had, and the bluest eyes. And I thought if she was going to the same place, I might see my Flora. I'd like to see her." She wiped her eyes with the back of her hand.

"And did you?" I asked, knowing the answer.

"No," she said.

"What did you see?"

"I followed her to Bagnigge Wells – I thought she might be meeting someone in the gardens there. But she crossed over the street and walked along next to the high wall of the prison, where the river runs..."

"The Fleet?" I asked. "Next to Coldbath Fields?"

She nodded. "She stopped, and I hid behind a tree. And then – she dropped the baby into the river."

"I suppose you thought," I said, turning to look at Marwood, "that if the baby was discovered, it would be assumed that some poor unfortunate in the prison had disposed of it."

"What else could I do with it?" she asked calmly, as though discussing an unwanted dog. "I've dropped plenty of little bastards into that river over the years." She looked at the maid. "Plenty."

There was a roar of rage and pain, and before I could react Matthews had flung herself upon her mistress and dragged her to the floor. By the time I separated them – and in all truth I did not rush to Marwood's aid – the older woman was missing a clump of hair and had four livid scratches down her face. And the younger, her chest heaving with sobs, had retreated into the darkness of knowing that little Flora was lost to her forever.

Something old, something blue

THURSDAY 29TH JUNE 1826

After a short and unsettled night's sleep in the foetid air, I was yawning widely at the table when there was a knock at the back door. Martha looked over her shoulder from the stove.

"That sounds like William to me – his nose will be twitching."

And indeed it was; I held the door open, and Wilson ducked into the kitchen.

"Good morning, Mrs Plank," he said, his eyes drawn to the bacon that was cooking on the range. "I thought Constable Plank might like company on his walk to the office."

Martha raised her eyebrows, but gestured to the table and Wilson sat down. We both knew that money was tight in the Wilson household, and that he often left home early so that his mother could share the meagre breakfast between her younger children, but if this pretence preserved his dignity, we were happy to play along.

"Sam has not yet had his breakfast, William," said Martha. "Can I tempt you to join him?"

"Only if you have enough, Mrs Plank," said Wilson politely.

"We always have enough for you, William," replied my wife, which was not strictly true; I knew that she would be handing over some of her portion to him. But women are born for caring and nurturing, and it would be foolish of me to interfere.

As we walked to the police office, I described for Wilson the events of the previous day, and what I had told Martha.

When I had finished, he said softly, "You cannot protect Mrs Plank from everything, sir."

"No," I agreed, "but like that wretched clerk Jamison, I must do all I can."

We walked on in silence. When we turned into Great Marlborough Street, he spoke again. "I've been thinking about the money. The takings from the blackmail. Where do you think it is?"

"In such situations, I usually find it easier to start with where it is not," I replied. We climbed the steps, nodded a greeting to Tom Neale who was doing his best to talk sense to a man who was as drunk as an emperor and in no mood to listen, and went into the back office. It had just gone nine, and any warrants that the magistrates might issue before their hearings at ten would soon start appearing.

"So where is the money not?" asked Wilson.

"Well, it is not with its rightful owners. And it is not with any of the thugs and bullies that Willoughby sends out with the collection plate; he will insist that they hand it over sharpish, before they're tempted to spend it in the tavern or the bawdy house. And it will not be at Willoughby's place of work; taking it into a police office would be too risky even for him."

"But it's not all his, is it?"

"Indeed not," I agreed. "Willoughby is the puppet, and payment goes to the puppet master."

"Percival," said Wilson spitting the word out. "But how does Willoughby get the money to Percival, and what does Percival do with it?"

"Two excellent questions," I said.

There was a knock at the door and Tom's head appeared, followed by a hand holding a warrant. "From Mr Dawson," he said. "Vagabonding, outside Webb's Hotel in Piccadilly – the keeper is complaining that guests are being importuned."

I stood and took it from him. "Best show willing," I said, putting on my hat. "And you," I turned to Wilson, "have a think about what we were discussing. It has to be somewhere, that money."

When I walked into the front office a couple of hours later, having delivered a miserable old man into the hands of the court clerk, Wilson was waiting.

"Thank heavens you're back, Sam," said Tom with a wink. "If you'd been much longer, he might have expired." And indeed Wilson was almost hopping from foot to foot with excitement, reminding me that, despite his great size, he was still a young man.

"I take it you've found something?" I asked as he led me to the back office.

"It was under our noses all the time," he said. "Here: I'll show you."

I sat at the table and he pushed towards me the jarvey's ledger. "After you'd gone, it occurred to me: might Thorpe have been involved with the money as well? After all, with a coach at his disposal, it would be an ideal way to move it around. So I went up to see Mr Conant and asked to have another look at this."

"Did he ask why?"

Wilson shook his head. "He was busy with his papers; he just took it out of his desk and gave it to me."

"And is there anything?"

Wilson reached over my shoulder and opened the book from the back. "Feel that back cover," he said, pointing. I did so; it was thick and padded. "Now feel the front cover." It was much thinner and harder. "Look." Wilson carefully peeled away the edge of the lining paper inside the back cover, and revealed a pocket between the two. "Feel inside there," he instructed me. I did so; there were some papers and I pulled them out. There were six sheets in total, folded in half, and each divided into columns.

I looked up at Wilson. "Just like a banking ledger," I said. "A record of money."

"Aye," he said, sitting down beside me. "That's the right-hand column – amounts of money. And the left-hand column is the date. But the two middle ones: hidden meanings again."

I shook my head. "Thorpe was certainly a careful man."

"But not that imaginative," said Wilson. "It's flowers again. So I went back up to Mr Conant's room..."

"You didn't bother him twice in a morning, I hope," I said.

"Oh no, I knew he was in court – Thin Billy took me in when I explained what I was after. He knew the book

I meant; he said that Miss Lily had not yet collected it and sure enough, it was there on the sideboard."

"And what has it revealed?"

"You see this entry: 18th March 1826, saxifrage, Michaelmas resemblance, 50 shillings."

I whistled through my teeth. "A fortnight's wage for a constable, that is – no trifling amount."

"Well, I wondered whether the two middle columns were where the money was collected, and where it was taken."

"And does it work?" I asked. "Can you decipher place names?"

"I can," he said with a wide smile. "Well, not all of them – not yet. But that one on 18th March – it said 'Michaelmas resemblance'. And that phrase appears quite often in the ledger, in both columns, so it must be important. It had me foxed for a while, and then I remembered Alice."

"Alice Godfrey?"

He nodded. "Well, 'Michaelmas resemblance' is nonsense until you break it into two different parts. And Phillips tells us," he turned to another marked page, "that the Michaelmas daisy is the emblem of cheerfulness in old age, while – and this one works the other way round, which was a bit confusing – resemblance is symbolised by the speedwell. A little blue flower. So we have something old, and something blue."

"Old Blue Boar Yard," I said quietly. "Just around the corner from the Blue Boar."

"There's a coachyard there," said Wilson. "They do repairs on the coaches, and make harnesses, as well as stabling the horses."

"And look," I said, pointing at the paper. "Lustre, again."

Wilson nodded. "Fair Maids of France. Mrs Marwood's establishment."

I sat back in my chair. "You've done excellent work, my lad." Wilson beamed. "And now we must find a way to get into that coachyard and see just what is going on."

CHAPTER THIRTY-FOUR

Moulding the law

FRIDAY 30TH JUNE 1826

The next day I was about to go out and see Jem Butler, to ask his advice on how to find out who at the coachyard might be willing to help me, when Tom Neale knocked on the office door.

"Upstairs," he said, jerking his head towards the ceiling. "And you're to take young Wilson with you."

Wilson looked up from his notebook; he had taken to heart the advice I had given him about starting each day by reviewing what he had written the previous day, and was paging through what we had seen on our casual perambulations around Old Blue Boar Yard the afternoon before.

"Tidy yourself, lad," I said, pointing to his unbuttoned coat. He quickly did so, and we went up the stairs to the magistrate's dining room. Conant called us in and invited me to sit; he knew better than to ask Wilson, who felt more comfortable standing.

"Constables," said the magistrate, "I thought you would like to know that I have come to a decision about the Brigstock matter. No, not the blackmail – I know you are still looking into that – but the death of Francis Brigstock. Since that unfortunate incident, I have had several long discussions with Edward Brigstock." I must have looked surprised. "Not here, no – but at my club, and once at Hans Place with Sir John." He paused as though searching for the right words. "Although the circumstances of the death could suggest manslaughter, I am minded to think it a tragic accident. The intent was to startle the man, not to hit the animal and make it bolt. And the remorse that Edward feels – and expresses – is both genuine and terrible. His father is now aware of all of the details of the incident, but his sister, Lily's friend Sophia, has been allowed to think it a simple riding accident, and there is little to be gained from disabusing her of this belief."

"Mr Conant," I said, "I will confess that I am a little uneasy."

"As I knew you would be, Sam, which is why I wanted to explain it to you. Sometimes we must adjust the means to achieve the correct ends." He leaned forward. "Do you believe that Edward Brigstock intended to kill his brother?" I shook my head. "Then that takes care of a charge of murder. Do you believe that Edward hit the horse by accident?" I nodded. "Then without a reckless but deliberate act, manslaughter would be hard to prove. Now, do you think that Edward has gained from the death of his brother – financially or in any other way?"

"Not as far as I can tell," I replied.

"I can assure you that he has not; as the eldest son, Edward's position was always secure, and he had nothing to gain from the death of a younger brother. More than that, I can tell you that he has lost a great deal: a much loved brother, a contented father, his own peace of mind. Until the day he dies, he will know that, had he not gone out riding with his brother that day, Francis Brigstock would still be alive. As he himself has told me, no punishment imposed by a court could match that."

"So you would be content for him to marry Miss Sheridan?" I asked.

The magistrate thought for a moment. "I do not think he would put her in any danger, if that's what you mean, but as for whether marriage to a man so filled with grief and guilt would be recommended – I may well have a discreet word with Izzy's father."

"But what of Croft – the groom?" asked Wilson.

"Ah yes, Croft," said Conant. "I have spoken to him and explained a little of what I have just said to you. He sees even more clearly than I that Edward Brigstock lives his remorse every day. A changed man, he called his master. And with Edward's confession to his father, the horse has been spared, which is a great relief to Croft." The magistrate stood and went to the window, glancing out into the street before turning to face us. "But I have not taken this decision purely out of compassion for Edward and his family. His father and I have struck a deal." He returned to his seat and leaned forward eagerly.

"Well, I think that is rather clever," said Martha that evening. "Influence is a marvellous thing, when turned to the right purpose."

"But that is not how it should work," I protested. "The purpose of the law is to present everyone with the same set of rules that will be applied in the same way, with the same results."

"Come now, Sam." My wife turned from the range and looked at me levelly. Relations between us had improved since my arrest of Mrs Marwood, but I knew that there was still work to be done. "Do I need to remind you that you are not above moulding the law a little when it suits you? I seem to remember that you did not haul Alice before the bench for prostitution."

I folded my arms and said nothing. Teaching a woman to be logical can have consequences.

"And surely this is a good outcome. It is a stroke of luck that Sir John Brigstock has an interest in chartering convict ships to the government, and an even greater stroke of luck that he can arrange for the Yates-Drummond boy to be taken on as assistant to the surgeon on one."

I took out my notebook. "The *Speke II*," I said. "Due to leave Sheerness in early August, bound for Port Jackson in New South Wales. Until then, we have Yates-Drummond's word that his son will be kept under close watch and schooled by a surgeon." I looked up at Martha. "It will not be an easy journey, even for those above decks."

"And no more it should be, for Mr Yates-Drummond," said Martha. "He is fortunate not to be facing the scaffold. Instead he will have hard work, a clean start away from the fast crowd he was running with here in London, and a chance for adventure."

I nodded. "It's certainly a great deal more than he cared to give Ellen."

CHAPTER THIRTY-FIVE

Counsel at the Saracen's Head

MONDAY 3RD JULY 1826

The matter was still troubling me on Monday morning and as she helped me on with my coat, Martha turned me to face her.

"Samuel Plank," she said, "if you ever tire of being a constable, you will make an admirable parson, carrying the weight of the world on your shoulders and your distress on your face." She reached up to kiss my cheek. "Go and talk to someone about your concerns – John Wontner, perhaps, or one of your lawyers. And come home to me this evening with a lighter heart. We both need that."

I walked down Norton Street, trying to keep in the shade of the buildings; a constable's uniform makes no allowance for sultry summers. When I reached Carburton

Street, I paused. Martha was right: turning it over in my own mind was pointless. I needed to lay the matter before someone whose opinion and judgement I trusted, someone who knew the law better than almost anyone. And instead of heading south towards Piccadilly and the police office, I turned my nose towards Holborn.

At number 87 Hatton Garden – a tall, fine building with black railings – I had just raised my hand to knock on the door when it was heaved open and I was nearly bowled over as James Harmer barrelled out.

"A thousand apologies," he called as he strode off down Hatton Garden. After a few yards he stopped and looked back. "Sam Plank?" he asked. "Constable Plank?" I nodded; it was nearly two years since we had last met, so his memory was impressive. "Come – walk with me. You will not be surprised to hear that I am late for an appointment. Newgate."

I had to trot to catch up with him; Mr Harmer, despite his considerable bulk, was an energetic walker, not least because – as he said – he was often late. We turned into Holborn.

"And how may I help you, constable?" he asked, looking quickly to one side and then the other before striding out across the thoroughfare, ushering me along with him and giving a cheery wave to a cart-driver who had to pull to a halt to let him pass. "You have some work for me? A hopeless case, as the news-sheets would have it?" He smiled; he knew of his well-deserved reputation for taking on lost souls and radical causes.

"Not this time, no," I smiled in return. "There is a matter – a matter of law – that is troubling me, and I could think of no better person to consult for guidance."

"In that case," said Harmer, drawing his watch from his pocket, "I think we will pause. My defendant, I fear, is not going anywhere, and he can wait a few more minutes before I tell him that. There: that will do – I feel in urgent need of refreshment." He glanced up Snow Hill and indicated the Saracen's Head.

Once we were settled with a tankard of ale in front of each of us, Harmer took a long draught, smacked his lips, leaned back with his arms crossed, and said, "Well?"

I explained as succinctly as I could, without giving any names of those involved; if Mr Harmer disagreed with our approach and decided to act on what he had heard, Mr Conant would not be best pleased. When I had finished, I looked across at the lawyer.

"To sum up," he said, as he must have said hundreds of times before, "we have two young gentlemen with connections: one the son of a war hero and the other the son of a Member of Parliament. Both implicated – one by his own admission and the other by a reliable witness – in the death of another." I nodded. "And it has been proposed that prosecuting the son of the war hero," I nodded again, "would achieve nothing except to cause further distress to him and his family – who are already mourning the loss of one son." He raised an eyebrow at me. "And that, I feel, is the nub of this particular case. Were the victim and the perpetrator unrelated, then I would be pressing for a judicial outcome in order for the family of the victim to see justice done. But it serves nothing to punish the family again; the loss of one son and the genuine remorse of the other is more than enough for them to bear."

I took a swallow of ale and considered. "And the other – the son of the honourable member?" I asked.

Harmer's face hardened. "This man is like so many of his fellows: spoilt, lacking in purpose or direction, and careless of others. He is certainly deserving of punishment. But putting him before the court would prove fruitless. The father may express his disgust at his son's behaviour, but I guarantee that were the matter to proceed, the man would throw the full weight of his influence behind making sure that any action did not succeed. He would call in every favour, make every threat at his disposal – and he would carry the day. His friends and acquaintances would rally around him, knowing that there but for the grace of God..." He drained his tankard and shook his head. "There would be no trial, constable, and certainly no conviction. In the circumstances, I would say that you have negotiated an excellent solution. This unlicked cub will find himself on a ship of horrors, heading for the other side of the world, where his connections and pretensions will be of little use to him. He will be in the company of men far more brutal and ruthless than himself. And he will live in fear of the convicts learning of his past; there is a strange chivalry among such men, and his callous treatment of that young girl will not work in his favour. More than likely, he will soon wish he had stayed to face a jury."

The bells of St Sepulchre's tolled the hour, and Harmer hauled himself to his feet. "I am sorry to leave you, constable, but duty calls: if I do not attend to my man, he may soon hear the great bell instead."

I nodded in understanding; too often I had heard the great bell of the church being rung to signify that a prisoner had been executed in the yard of Newgate.

The lawyer tucked his satchel under his arm and held out his hand. "We are men of ideals, you and I, constable, but we must learn which battles to fight and which to leave."

"Thank you for your counsel, sir," I said. "It has gone a good way to settling my mind."

"I am thankful that there are men like you, with minds to be unsettled by such circumstances," said Harmer. "The more we think, the more we question, and the more we question, the more we improve." It was as good a motto as any I had heard, and I raised my tankard in salute.

CHAPTER THIRTY-SIX

Horses and bears

WEDNESDAY 5TH JULY 1826 – MORNING

The horses stepped and whinnied as they heard us opening the gate of Old Blue Boar Yard. Clouds roiled and tumbled above us, but mercifully the rain had stopped for a while. I glanced up at the hayloft over the stables where the lad Stephens would be sleeping, but a few coins from me and the promise from Mr Atkins of a generous breakfast at the Blue Boar had guaranteed that he would not look out, even if he woke.

We trod carefully, trying to keep our balance; the rags we had tied over our boots muffled their sound but also made them much more slippery on the wet stones. The cobbled yard was tidy, with only one coach in for repairs; it stood to one side, traces off and with one wheel missing, the axle propped up on blocks of wood. I tapped Wilson on the arm, and indicated by pointing that he should look in the stables while I inspected the coach.

I looked all around the outside of the cab. Traces of a fine coat of arms could just be seen – and, with the tips of the fingers, felt – on the door panels; no doubt the family that had once commissioned such a grand conveyance had, like so many, fallen on hard times. Much of London's fleet of hackneys consists of coaches with similar grand pedigrees, but the original livery is always quickly painted over to spare the blushes of the original owners. The box at the front, where the jarvey would perch, was missing its cushion; this was standing propped against the front wheel, and – to judge by the straw poking through the hessian cover – was awaiting patching and re-stuffing.

After checking the outside of the coach, I leaned against it and rocked it gently to check that it was stable on the three wheels and the pile of blocks. It seemed firm. I opened the door, put my foot on the step and climbed in. The upholstery maker was obviously in the middle of his work. Both long seat cushions were missing, and someone had drawn chalk marks on the bare wooden benches to indicate where nails should be knocked back in and rough edges sanded down. In the dim light I crouched and felt around on the floor of the coach – searching for what, I was not sure. I worked my hands up the sides of the bench seats, where thin pads of horse-hair were tacked in place to buffer the passengers from the harsher jolting of their journey. And as I pressed on one of these pads, I noticed that it felt different – less springy, flatter, as though it was missing its innards. As I worked my fingers along the top of the pad, I realised that it was not sewn shut, but laced with a cord. I knelt down and felt for the end of the cord, pulling it loose about four or five inches from the corner. I then leaned forward and worked my hand down into the pad – and touched what felt like paper. Folded paper. I twisted myself into a better position, and strained with the very tips of my fingers to get a purchase. Just as cramp was threatening, I was able to pinch the paper and pull it out of the pad. I turned it to the faint dawn light that was just straying into the courtyard. It was a pound note, drawn on the Weymouth and Dorsetshire Bank. I was leaning forward again, to see if there were more notes hidden in the pad, when I heard a creak as someone else stepped into the coach. Expecting Wilson, I turned with a smile and was just able to get my arm up before I was hit over the head and fell senseless to the floor.

When I woke, I was propped up in a chair in the corner of the yard. I tried to raise a hand to my pounding temple and realised that both hands were tied behind me. Standing looking down at me, legs planted wide and thumbs hooked into the pockets of his waistcoat, was a bear of a man. To judge from the vivid description that young Stephens had given us, this was the coachyard owner Mr Connors. Seeing me wake, he jerked his chin at me.

"That lump on your noggin will be a reminder to you not to go ferreting where you don't belong," he said.

I nodded, and it felt as though my brain was loose in my skull so I stopped again.

"I don't take kindly to thieves in my yard – not kiddies and not a square toes like you. Now, what were you looking for?"

I licked my lips. "Anything I can sell," I croaked, every word making my head throb. I mimicked the old salts I remembered from Wapping, doing what they could to find money for the next drink. "I'm partial, see. Partial to me drink. I saw the coach, and thought there might be a coin or two dropped down the side. Just enough to get me chirping merry." I looked up at him slyly.

"Chirping merry!" snorted Connors. "You're an old toper if ever I saw one. And this would have bought you a good few drams, wouldn't it?" He extracted the pound note from his pocket and waved it in front of me before carefully folding it and tucking it away again. "Well, if it's liquid refreshment you're after, you'll get a bellyful soon. A bellyful of Thames water." He gave me a nasty smile.

Behind him, I could see the stable door opening slowly. I tried to distract him.

"Have mercy on a miserable soul, sir, what's never had much luck in life," I snivelled.

"And what little you did have has run out now, hasn't it, old man?" he said.

Just then there was a terrible clattering of hooves and neighing and whinnying as half a dozen horses broke out of the stables and swarmed into the yard. Unused to being out of harness and without a man to lead them, they rolled their shining eyes in terror and barged into each other, their shoes slipping on the rain-slicked cobbles.

"What the..." cried Connors, turning to the swirling crowd of horses. "Boy!" he roared. "Boy! The horses are out!" I saw a tousled head look down from the hayloft. Behind me I could feel someone tugging at the cords on my wrists; looking down, I saw Wilson on his hands and knees. He must have crawled out of the stable after releasing the horses.

Connors spotted him at the same moment. With a bellow of anger he plucked a bridle from a hook on the stable wall and swung it around his head like a slingshot; the metal bit whistled alarmingly as it cut through the air and I leaned away, bracing myself. Just then there was a terrific clap of thunder and one of the horses took fright, rearing up, hooves flailing. It skittered on the cobbles and crashed back down, on top of Connors. He collapsed to the floor with a groan and then was silent.

"Is he...?" I asked.

Wilson stood and walked over to him, crouching to check by lifting one of his eyelids. "Yes," he said. "I don't think it was the horse, though – he hit his head on the stones. There's plenty of blood."

I heard a whimper and saw Stephens peering round the door.

"Get a knife, lad, and cut these cords behind me," I said in as normal a voice as I could muster. He nodded and ducked back into the stable, returning a few moments later to release me. The rope had drawn blood from one of my wrists and my shoulders were both wrenched from when Connors had hauled me into the chair and tied me up, but I wasn't too bad.

Wilson took my elbow and helped me to stand. He peered at my forehead. "I don't know what Mrs Plank is going to say about that lump," he said. I felt it gingerly with my fingertips and winced.

"I do," I said, "but I'll blame it all on you. I'll say you were tied to the chair and I had to rescue you."

"Let go of me, woman," I gasped. The moment Wilson was out of the door Martha had grabbed hold of me and hugged me so tightly I could barely breathe.

"Did it not occur to you for one moment, Samuel Plank, that you might be discovered?" She held me at arm's-length and narrowed her eyes at me. "Is that why you told me that fib about following the money? So that I wouldn't worry, or try to stop you?"

"We were following the money," I said in protest. "We knew the coachyard was significant and I was trying to find out why."

"You know very well that I thought you were following the money in Thorpe's ledger – sitting in that nice dry back office with Wilson, and Tom Neale bringing you tea."

"Talking of which..." I said.

She rolled her eyes, but turned to the range. "Now you get upstairs and out of those filthy clothes, and when you come back down you can have a wash and some breakfast."

By the time I came back downstairs she had been as good as her word: a bowl of hot water sat on the table, a flannel draped over the edge, and the tempting smell of bacon came from the oven. I washed carefully, trying not to grimace as I touched my scrapes and bruises, and Martha passed me a warmed towel. I slipped my shirt on and sat down to eat.

"So what did you find?" asked Martha as I was mopping up the bacon fat with my bread.

I smiled at her. "I knew you couldn't resist," I said.

"Just for that," she said archly, taking my empty plate, "I'm going to give your second helping of bacon to the dog."

"We don't have a dog," I pointed out.

"I'll get one, and save the bacon for him." She opened the warming oven and loaded up my plate again. "Unless you care to stop your teasing and tell me."

The bacon in front of me, I explained about finding the pound note in the side cushion of the coach.

"And when the surgeon came to deal with Connors, Wilson and I went back to the coach to look for more money, but there was nothing there. We were either too late or too early – the pound note I found was the only one."

"That's a pity," said Martha.

"Aye, but at least now we know how they move the money around. No-one bats an eyelid at seeing a coach rattling about the place, stopping here, waiting there. And if the jarvey happens to be inside it between fares, tidying the cushions, well, so he should." I held out my cup and Martha refilled it. "And it's not just around London. We found record books in the coachyard, and several of their coaches have been sold on to buyers on the Continent – France, and Prussia. Who knows: maybe some of the money went with them."

Martha shook her head. "And all of it made from other people's misery."

CHAPTER THIRTY-SEVEN

Spelt as it sounds

WEDNESDAY 5TH JULY 1826 – AFTERNOON

Mr Conant looked at me with amusement. "You look as though you've gone a few rounds with Tom Cribb," he said.

"I feel like it too," I said, carefully touching the lump on my forehead.

"A pity you didn't find more of the money," said the magistrate, glancing down at the pound note I had handed him.

"We think the coach was being prepared for another journey," I said, "and the note I found had been left behind from a previous job. Mr Connors had plenty of coaches in and out of that yard. I'm going to call in at the Hackney Coach Office near the Strand – Mr Atkins at the Blue Boar suggested it."

"To check that Mr Connors holds the correct licences for his coaches?"

"Indeed; Mr Atkins seemed to think that we might find out something interesting, as he had heard rumours of complaints against Mr Connors. It may be nothing, but at the very least we shall be able to know for certain how many coaches are – were – under his control."

"I shall be here until late this evening," said the magistrate as I stood to leave. "My daughter is holding a card evening and hot supper at home and I have no desire to find myself called in to make up a table. Come and see me if you find out anything from the coach commissioners."

The Hackney Coach Office had just re-opened, and I was among the first callers of the afternoon. A junior clerk asked my business and when I explained that I was a constable making enquiries on behalf of a magistrate, he looked over his shoulder at an older man behind the counter. He in turn pointed his pen to a door at the side, and I was shown into a small private office. A moment later, the more senior clerk joined me. He looked askance at the state of my face and indicated that I should sit on one side of the table while he took the chair on the other. He opened a book, dipped his pen, and looked up at me.

"And you are Constable..." he said, waiting.

"Plank," I supplied, "Samuel Plank."

"Spelt as it sounds?" he asked, writing carefully.

"Exactly," I said.

"And you wish to enquire about one of our licensees?"

I nodded. "Mr William Connors, of Old Blue Boar Yard."

"Spelt as it sounds?" he asked again.

"I imagine so, yes," I replied.

He wrote in a beautiful hand, to be sure, but the effort took some time.

"And which of these forms the basis of your concern, constable?" asked the clerk. He turned to the front of his book and extracted a loose piece of paper and handed it to me.

I read it – it seemed to be a list of possible complaints that one could make. 'Coachman, behaviour or language of: rude, abusive, insulting, dishonest, disrespectful. Fare: unreasonable, not as agreed, refused without good reason. Property: stolen, lost, damaged. Coach: dirty, overcrowded, late for booking, in poor repair, unlicensed. Horse/s: unkempt, poorly treated, over-whipped, underheight (fourteen hands or less), over/under-fed.'

"Well, none of them, actually," I said, returning the paper to the clerk. "Mr Connors has recently died," the clerk looked solemn, and carefully inscribed a crucifix next to Connors' name in his notes, "and I am making enquiries about his licences."

"The licences of a licensee form part of his estate and as such pass to his heirs," recited the clerk. "If those heirs

292 | SUSAN GROSSEY

continue to pay the carriage tax, the licence shall be maintained."

"I am more interested in how Mr Connors conducted his business while he was alive. I have been told that there were complaints against him – you obviously do receive complaints at this office." I gestured at the sheet of paper, which the clerk hastily slipped back into his book. "Would it be possible for me to see any records you have pertaining to him?"

The clerk sniffed, perhaps considering whether my question could be considered 'behaviour: impertinent' or 'request: unreasonable'. "Wait here, if you please," he said, standing. "William Connors, you say?"

I nodded. "Spelt as it sounds."

A few minutes later the clerk returned with a small bundle of papers tied with a ribbon. He sat down and untied them.

"There have been six complaints made about coaches and coachmen connected with Mr Connors," said the clerk, "but over a period of nearly three years, this is not excessive."

"Serious complaints?" I asked, leaning forward to look at the papers. The clerk slid them out of my reach.

"Not serious, no – although Mr Connors was summoned to this office some eight months ago when we received a third complaint of his coaches being dirty. He assured us that the matter would be attended to, and since then, nothing."

"Three years, you said?" I asked. "Mr Connors was granted his first licence three years ago?"

"Nearly three years," corrected the clerk. He sifted through the papers. "Yes, here we are: Mr William Connors, recommended for a hackney coach licence by a magistrate."

"May I see that?" I held out my hand.

"It is perfectly in order," said the clerk defensively. "No person may obtain a licence to possess a hackney coach unless he is recommended by a peer, a Member of Parliament or some other influential being. Often a gentleman will recommend a former servant. And a magistrate would certainly be considered an influential being."

I sat with my hand outstretched, and eventually and with great reluctance the clerk passed me the paper. It was an application for a licence, dated 9th September 1823. At the top was the applicant's name – William Connors – and below that a space where he could state the number of hackney coaches he wished to buy. Connors had started out with two, it seems. And below that was written the name and office of the man who had recommended him: Henry Dawson Esquire, magistrate of Great Marlborough Street. Another "special verdict", no doubt.

CHAPTER THIRTY-EIGHT

The ways of the world

THURSDAY 13TH JULY 1826

As we stood outside the bank a week later, Martha's grip tightened on my arm. She was not a nervous woman – far from it – but the prospect of finally meeting Edward Freame had unsettled her. She knew a great deal about him from me, and understood that I held him in very high esteem, but when I told her that he had requested an introduction, she was almost speechless – a rare condition for my wife.

"Well!" she had said when I had reported his invitation, dropping down into a chair in the kitchen and looking around her, as though an explanation might fall out of the walls or cupboards. "Why on earth would a Quaker banker want to meet me?"

"I doubt it's anything to do with his religion or profession, Martha, but he was most insistent. Maybe he simply wants to thank you for the assistance you gave Alice and Ellen; after all, they were nominally under the care of a charity with which Mr Freame is associated."

She considered this. "Hmmm, yes, perhaps that is it. Just that. Indeed. Well, I shall need new gloves."

And it was one of those new gloves that grasped me so tightly now. A nearby church struck nine, and as though propelled by the sound, the banker walked briskly around the corner. When he saw us, he smiled widely and swept off his hat in an almost theatrical gesture, bowing to my wife.

"Mrs Plank, Mrs Plank," he said warmly, "our very first meeting – the first of many, I hope – and already I am in the wrong. I had every intention of arriving early to prepare for you, but an overturned dray put paid to that – the horse was lamed, the lad inconsolable. What could I do but stop to help? Your husband will have told you that I am a shockingly sentimental man." Martha said nothing – indeed Freame allowed her no time to say anything – but her grip on my arm loosened. "And now here I am, keeping you in the street when you must be in need of refreshment."

With that, he led us through the front door into the banking hall, calling good morning to his staff, and on into the parlour. He took care to give Martha the most comfortable of the chairs, and chattered away at her until he was sure that there was nothing more that he could supply for her ease. Only once she was installed with her feet on a stool, a cup of tea in one hand and a Prince of Wales biscuit in the other, did the banker sit back in his own chair and get down to business.

"I am sure you have both been wondering why I asked so specifically to meet Mrs Plank – apart from, of course, to verify for myself that such a paragon as described by the constable here could actually exist."

Martha looked at me in astonishment.

"Mr Freame is teasing you – or perhaps me," I said. "I am afraid that our discussions are usually much less pleasant than that."

Freame's face became more serious. "Your husband is right, Mrs Plank. Sadly, he and I rarely have the opportunity to talk of the more enjoyable aspects of life. But occasionally we do manage to create something worthwhile out of despair, and this is exactly what I hope you will help me to do."

"Mr Freame," said Martha, finding her voice at last, "my husband holds you in extremely high regard, both as a friend and as a professional man. He has told me of your charitable works, and I know he values your expertise and opinion. If I can help to repay his – our – debt to you, I will be delighted."

Freame shook his head. "Madam, there is no question at all of debt. Your husband and I have collaborated in our common desire to see good rewarded." He looked at me and I inclined my head in acknowledgement. "But now I have had an idea for which both he and I are entirely unsuited, and so I turn to you."

Over the next half-hour, Freame laid out his plan. He talked of the house on Harrison Street, gallantly sparing Martha the details of what had gone on there, but then of course I, being both less gallant and more in need of her understanding, had already told her everything. Well, almost everything.

"Having discussed the matter carefully, my fellow committee members and I have agreed to continue providing financial support to Harrison Street, but with some significant changes. It has been decided that it will become a home for young unwed mothers and their babies. What your husband has told me about... Alice, was it," Martha and I both nodded, "and the second girl..."

"Ellen," said Martha.

Freame nodded. "Ellen, yes. Heart-breaking. What I have learnt about the difficulties faced by these poor girls has convinced me of the need to provide a safe haven for them, somewhere they can go to await the arrival of their babies, and where they can stay for perhaps six months afterwards as they look for work and a steady position. Why, Mrs Plank, have I upset you?"

The banker leaned forward in concern, as Martha dabbed at her eyes and shook her head.

"I very much hope you approve of my plans, Mrs Plank, as I particularly need your help with what comes next."

Martha looked at me, but I was at much at sea as she.

"In order for a house like this to flourish, for it to provide the girls with more than just a few months' lodging, it must give them the skills and confidence to move into motherhood with pride and dignity. Of course we need a reliable and kindly woman to live in with them," Freame saw me about to say something and held up his hand to halt me, "but I would not presume to ask the constable here to give up his wife, no matter how worthy the cause. In fact, I have found the ideal woman already; Mrs Anderson is a war widow, with four grown children of her own, and exactly the kind of practical, caring soul we need. And the maid Matthews is staying on.

"But – and here I turn at last to you, Mrs Plank – Mrs Anderson has her limitations. She is not an educated woman, nor indeed a worldly one. And I want the girls – the young women – who leave our house to be both literate and, how can I put this, shrewd. Canny, even. For if they are to stay on a steady path, they need to be aware of the dangers lurking in the undergrowth. I am not one of those men who thinks that women are best protected by keeping them ignorant." He paused. "Your husband tells me that you can read and write, Mrs Plank." Martha nodded. "He also – and you will have to forgive him for this – tells me that over many years of marriage, he has shared with you many of the more unpleasant situations he has encountered."

"I would not wish it otherwise," said Martha stoutly. "If Sam can stand it, so can I."

"Excellent, excellent," said Freame. "So my proposal is this. While the girls are living at Harrison Street, Mrs Anderson will teach them to care for their babies, along with cookery and needlework – so many of these girls lack maternal instruction, as you both know. But to prepare them for employment and life beyond Harrison Street, Mrs Plank, I would very much like you to run regular instruction in reading and writing, and in what we might call social and moral education. The ways of the world, perhaps."

Whatever I had expected to hear at Freame's bank that morning, this was not it. I had never heard of such a programme of reform, such a clear-thinking and practical proposal, but I knew instantly that it could work. And the shining look of excitement on Martha's face showed that she was in agreement.

"Well, Mrs Plank?" asked Freame. "Might you be interested?"

CHAPTER THIRTY-NINE

A desperate man

FRIDAY 14TH JULY 1826

"**M**r Freame's plan is for Mrs Plank to give instruction during the afternoons, while the babies rest in the care of Mrs Anderson," I concluded.

Mr Conant smiled. "It sounds like the perfect employment for your wife, and please do tell her that if she wishes to borrow any of my books to read to the girls," he indicated his crowded bookshelves with a sweep of his arm, "I should be delighted." His face became more serious. "Sit down, Sam, please." I did so. "Doubtless you have heard chatter downstairs this morning."

"Not chatter so much, sir – perhaps concerned speculation." The magistrate looked at me with a raised eyebrow. "Aye, chatter," I conceded.

"What I can confirm, constable, and you can share this information with the others, is that Mr Dawson has resigned his post as magistrate. His wife is in poor health and would benefit from a milder climate; she has a sister married to a wine merchant in Madeira, and the Dawsons have decided to join them out there. They set sail tomorrow. What you should know – and I leave it to you to decide who else needs to know this – is that I gave Mr Dawson little choice in the matter. I presented him with what we – you – had found out about his undeserved leniency in certain matters, his unwillingness to pursue the Yates-Hammond boy, and his recommendation for Connors to be given a hackney coach licence. I then told him of your discovery in the coachyard. And I asked him to commit to paper his understanding of the structure of the conspiracy – in particular the role of Mr Percival. An insurance policy, if you will, against Mr Dawson telling a different story later. He is a weak and unprincipled man but not a stupid one, and he was quick to see his way out."

"But does he deserve a way out?" I asked, trying not to sound like a spoilt child.

Conant nodded in sympathy. "Were Dawson acting alone, I too would prefer to see him face justice. But he is not acting alone, and we must sacrifice our desire to punish him so that we can be sure to trap Percival. It is not exactly transportation to Van Diemen's Land, but Dawson's banishment to Madeira is an exile. He will lose his status, and I will drop a few careful words in a few hungry ears; his new acquaintances in Madeira will soon learn that he left England under a cloud. For a man like Dawson, with few personal qualities to recommend him and even fewer internal resources to fall back on, you can rest assured that his inevitable isolation is a punishment that he will feel keenly."

"And Mr Percival?" I said. "May I ask how you propose to deal with him?"

Mr Conant sat back in his chair and steepled his hands. "An altogether more difficult situation," he said, frowning. "He is a far more cunning adversary than Dawson, with much more to lose, and therefore more dangerous. If we corner him, as I did Dawson, this man will fight to the death. And so I think, with Mr Percival, we must follow the rules and observe all the niceties. I have made an appointment to see the Lord Chancellor on Monday, and will lay before him everything we have learned about both Mr Percival and Mr Willoughby."

"And let the law take its course," I said.

"Indeed, constable. Indeed."

As I walked up Great Portland Street, a flower seller was packing up his barrow.

"Something pretty for the wife, constable?" he called as I passed. "Say sorry for whatever it is you've done wrong today." He winked at me. "We've always done something wrong, eh?"

When I walked into the kitchen, Martha was laying the table. She proffered her cheek and I kissed it.

"And as well as a kiss, there's this," I said, holding out the posy.

She took the flowers from me and held them to her nose. "How lovely, Sam," she breathed. "And I see that all those hours with Mr Phillips and his emblems have taught you something."

I turned from hanging up my coat. "Taught me something?"

She filled a vase with water and put the flowers into it, standing back to admire the little arrangement.

"Stocks," she said, indicating the blooms. "Signifying lasting beauty."

"Of course," I said quickly. "Lasting beauty. Which you have in abundance."

Martha laughed. "I know you, Samuel Plank – you bought whatever looked prettiest, with a few pennies off at the end of the day." I walked over and put my arm around her. "But they are lovely." She hugged me in turn. "You're lucky he wasn't selling off bunches of French willow." I looked at her, puzzled. "French willow," she repeated, "signifying celibacy."

After dinner we had just cleared the table when there was a loud rapping at the front door that made us both jump. Martha looked at me and I shrugged; we both knew that Wilson and the message lads would come to the back. I pulled back the bolt and opened the door; it was Jem Butler. I looked past him and his coach was in the street, so he was at work.

"Jem Butler," I said over my shoulder to Martha. "The jarvey."

"Well, bring him in," she said. "He'll need a warming drink at this time of night."

"I won't, thank you all the same," said Jem, twisting his hat in his hands and looking very uneasy. "I'm supposed to be waiting for a fare in Fitzroy Square, but I heard something that I thought you should know." He glanced over his shoulder and then leaned forward. "There's been an incident," he said quietly. "An accident. I heard about it from one of the other jarveys; he saw it and it'll be in the news-sheets tomorrow, but I thought you'd want to know right away." He checked over his shoulder again then turned back to me, his voice dropping even more – I had to lean forward to hear him. "This jarvey was waiting on the stand in Leather Lane when he heard a commotion. He looked around, and a curricle came at speed out of Charles Street. It was going too fast for the corner and it almost tipped over. As the driver calmed the horses before setting off again, the jarvey recognised him." Jem looked yet again over his shoulder. "It was Mr Percival, the magistrate."

I heard Martha gasp; she had crept to my side and was listening intently.

"There's more," said Jem urgently. "The commotion the jarvey heard before that. It turns out that several people said that the curricle had been whipped into a gallop deliberately, the other side of Hatton Garden, and then driven right across the street, knocking down a lad who was crossing at the time. It was a clerk from the same police office as Mr Percival – John Willoughby."

"Is he dead?" whispered Martha.

Jem shook his head. "Not dead, no, Mrs Plank, but badly injured. He's in St Bartholomew's." The jarvey put on his hat. "And now I must be off; if my fare comes out and I'm not there, I'll be in trouble." He touched his forehead and disappeared out into the darkness. I closed and bolted the door.

"Poor Mrs Thorpe," said Martha, sitting down heavily at the table. "First one son murdered, and now this happens to the second. You must go and see her tomorrow morning, Sam – it may be that no-one else will think to tell her."

I nodded. "But first I should call on Willoughby; he may be more inclined to help us now that Percival has turned on him."

CHAPTER FORTY

Cherries and wheat

SATURDAY 15TH JULY 1826

The shape lying under the sheet was barely recognisable as a man. Several broken bones, according to the elderly pockmarked woman who called herself a nurse and showed us to the right bed – broken bones, a cracked skull, and unknown internal injuries. From the way she shook her head and pressed her crucifix to her lips, I could tell that she did not expect John Willoughby to last much longer.

There was one chair near the bed and I pulled it closer and sat down, while Wilson looked about him and fetched a chair from further down the room. We looked at each other across the patient.

I cleared my throat. "Mr Willoughby?" I said quietly. "John Willoughby?"

The man stirred, and one swollen eye opened. "Aye," he said thickly.

"I am Constable Plank, and this is Constable Wilson."

He tried to say something. I spied a beaker of water on the bedside cabinet and lifted it to his lips. He craned forward to drink a little before letting his head fall back onto the pillow. "Great Marlborough Street," he said.

"Indeed." I put the beaker down.

Willoughby turned his head and looked at Wilson. "I know you – both of you. Seen you..." he swallowed with difficulty, "before. Serle's."

Wilson nodded. "That's right. When you met Edward Brigstock. And he called you an errand boy."

Willoughby turned his head again to look up at the ceiling. "He was right," he said after a moment. "Just an errand boy."

I leaned forward into his line of sight. "We know that, Mr Willoughby – we know that it was not your idea, not your scheme. And we know whose scheme it was. Do you?"

Wilson opened his notebook; it would be important to record exactly what Willoughby said.

Willoughby nodded. "Harmon Percival Esquire. Magistrate." He paused and looked straight at me. "My father."

"Your father?" I repeated.

"Ha!" said Willoughby, a rattle in his throat turning into a cough. The nurse looked over at us, and I reached again for the beaker of water. When Willoughby had recovered a little, he continued. "So you didn't know that, even with all your prying and following." I shook my head. "He won't come here when they tell him at Hatton Garden on Monday, about the unfortunate accident involving his clerk – won't risk people finding out."

Wilson looked at me and I stared back at him, willing him to stay silent. He did. What would be the point in telling a dying man that his own father had run him down rather than risk exposure?

"So if you and Gil Thorpe were half-brothers, but you had different mothers..." I spoke my thoughts aloud.

"Aye. Gil was another of Mr Percival's by-blows." Even through the injuries and the senses dulled with pain I could hear the bitterness in his voice. "As you surely know by now, my father, the well-respected magistrate, the Yorkshire squire and landowner, likes young girls." He drew in a ragged breath and his voice grew weaker, but he seemed determined to tell his story. He too knew his time was short. "My own mother was only fourteen when I was born. And Gil's mother was even younger, and so tiny that she died giving birth to him. But my mother was – is – so besotted with my father that she agreed to take in the baby Gil and bring him up alongside me as her own. And I loved him." I went to put my hand on his in comfort, but he drew it away from me. "She even changed her name from Willoughby to Thorpe to make the story ring true. And it worked: everyone felt sorry for the poor widow, two dead husbands and a young son from each."

"But there was no Mr Thorpe?" asked Wilson, his pencil scribbling across the page of his notebook.

"Nor any Mr Willoughby, come to that. A joke of sorts," said Willoughby. "My father's idea. It's the name of a village in Yorkshire, seat of the Percival family. Thorpe Willoughby." A tear made its way down his damaged face. "Poor Gil. Caught up like I was. We both made the mistake of doing whatever our father demanded of us, trying to please him – when in truth nothing pleases him. Nothing..." Wilson and I both leaned closer to catch what he was saying, "...but money."

As though this awful realisation had drained the last ounce of his determination, Willoughby closed his eyes. He sank, if it were possible, even further into the mattress, and his breathing became more laboured and terrible to hear. I turned to beckon the nurse. She bustled over and pushed past me to peer at her patient. She leaned in close, her ear to his mouth. Then she stood up and pulled the sheet over his face.

"Thank the Lord for His mercy," she said. She turned to look at me. "Does he have a wife? A mother? She should be told."

The heavy weather had finally broken and it was the sweetest summer's day as we walked to Clerkenwell. In Bowling Tree Lane the cherry trees that we had so admired the previous month were now laden with fruit and I plucked a few to slip into my pocket for Martha. We stopped outside Mrs Thorpe's house.

"This is a harsh errand," said Wilson. "How can we tell a mother for a second time that her son is dead?" He knocked. There was no reply. He knocked more loudly. The door of the neighbouring house opened and a woman looked out.

"If you're looking for Mrs Thorpe," she said, "you've missed her."

"Thank you," I said. "It is very important that we speak to her. Do you know when she might return?"

The neighbour folded her arms. "You've mistaken me. She's gone – gone for good. A coach came for her in the middle of the night – one of those fancy ones. And a man – distinguished-looking, he was. I saw him loading a few bits and pieces and then she came out with her bags and what not, and off they went. Nice to get some peace and quiet, after all that banging last night." She sniffed and went back indoors.

Wilson and I looked at each other. We tried the door of Mrs Thorpe's house and it opened. In the front room, it looked as though a very thorough search had been conducted: floorboards were levered up, cupboards standing open, drawers pulled out.

"A robbery?" asked Wilson.

I looked around again and then shook my head. "It's not messy enough. No, this is planned – done by someone who knows where everything is and is simply retrieving it."

Wilson walked through into the kitchen, and then ducked his head to climb the narrow staircase.

"It's the same up here," he called down. "Everything gone through."

I moved a pile of linen from one of the small armchairs and sat down. Wilson came back into the room.

"Well," I said, "I wonder how long Percival will shelter her. Now that he's reclaimed the money, he won't have much use for her any more – unless she can convince him she knows where there's more money hidden away."

"Or that she knows where the ledger is," said Wilson. "Percival will be keen to keep that out of the wrong hands." He stopped. "That's it: saxifrage." I looked at him questioningly. "From the ledger. Saxifrage signifies maternal love, and I couldn't for the life of me understand what it meant in terms of a location. And this is what it meant: money hidden in his mother's house."

"Poor woman," I said. "They all used her, didn't they? First Percival, then both of her sons, and now Percival again." I sighed. "And after all the flowers we've been following, it seems the only plant that matters is wheat."

"Wheat?" asked Wilson.

I looked around me at the deserted room. "Wheat: the emblem for riches."

Conant handed me the glass. "When swallowing a bitter pill," he said, raising his own glass to me, "I find that cognac helps it to slip down."

I nodded and drank, but said nothing.

Conant looked at me. "Perhaps I should have gone to the Lord Chancellor when we first had our doubts about Percival," he said, more as a question than a statement.

I stared into my glass. "Perhaps. But then the Lord Chancellor would have had a word with him, and Thorpe and Willoughby would have disappeared back into the woodwork."

"And instead they are both wearing wooden surcoats." The magistrate smiled grimly at me.

"And Mr Percival has escaped justice, amply funded," I said, not troubling to hide the bitterness in my voice.

Conant leaned over with the decanter and topped up my glass and then his own. "But what a price he has paid," he said. "His reputation in tatters, the murders of two sons on his conscience, his wife and legitimate son abandoned to face the censure of their neighbours – I doubt the man will have a peaceful night's sleep this side of the grave." He swallowed. "And all is not lost, Sam – Percival has escaped, he has not vanished. He will stumble one day, and we will be there to catch him by the elbow."

We both sat in silence as we contemplated this future pleasure.

"I hear that Mrs Marwood is to be removed to Newgate this afternoon," I said after a few moments.

Conant nodded and raised his glass again. "Now there is a success, Sam. Mrs Plank must be pleased to know that the wretched woman will never harm another child." He looked across at me and narrowed his eyes. "What is it? Is something troubling you?"

I put my glass on the side table and leaned forward, clasping my hands. "I did tell Martha, of course, that Marwood had been arrested. But," I looked up at Conant, "with our... difficulties, I had not the heart to tell her everything."

Conant waited, then prompted me. "You'd better tell me what she knows, so that I don't get you into trouble if she ever asks me about it."

I took a deep breath. "When Marwood was first arrested and taken to Coldbath Fields, I said that she had appeared before you and confessed to sending Ellen out with a man known for his violence, knowing that Ellen was still weak from childbirth. I told Martha that you had committed her for manslaughter." The magistrate raised an eyebrow but said nothing. "How could I tell her the rest?" I asked. "How could I tell a woman who has longed for a child for thirty years of the murder of two babies?" I looked down at my hands.

"So what does Mrs Plank think happened to Ellen's baby?" asked Conant quietly.

"I told her," I began, "I told her that he had been taken in by the Foundling Hospital."

"But surely she knows that they take in only children whose mothers are of good character," said Conant. "And Ellen was hardly that."

"I said that you had persuaded them to make an exception, that you had argued that Ellen's fall from grace was forced upon her, not chosen."

"And Mrs Plank believed you?"

I nodded.

"Are you sure? After all, the maid Matthews knows the poor child's fate, and she may have told Alice or even Mrs Plank." I looked up at the magistrate. "It would not surprise me," said Conant gently, "if it turns out that she already knows the truth but seeks to spare your feelings by allowing you to protect her." He smiled at me. "I may have been a widower for many years, Sam, but some lessons are learnt early on in a marriage." He drained his glass. "And one day, I am sure, you will be able to tell your wife that, thanks to your efforts, Mrs Marwood did face justice."

And he was right. Percival might have bought himself a few more months or years of restless freedom, but a blackmailer of necessity makes many enemies – and one day they will betray him. And what Martha had yet to learn from me was that Conant had committed Marwood not for manslaughter but for murder, and that now she was facing not just Newgate but also the noose.

Glossary

Abbess – the madam of a brothel

Ague – (or Covent Garden ague), gonorrhoea

Ape-drunk – very drunk

Barque of frailty – a young, attractive prostitute

Bawd – a female procuress, the mistress of a brothel

Bawdy house – a brothel

Beadle – originally a minor parish officer dealing with petty offenders, and since opening in 1819 the fashionable Burlington Arcade has been patrolled by its own beadles in smart uniforms

Bird of paradise – a prostitute

Bobbish – smart, spruce, well turned-out

Bon ton – high society, the fashionable elite

By-blow – an illegitimate child

Cart load – when someone grew very fat, it was said that they had fallen from a horse load to a cart load, i.e. they had become too heavy to ride a horse

Chirping merry – pleasantly tipsy and exhilarated

Clip the King's English – to be too drunk to speak clearly

Constable – an officer working for a magistrates' court, whose main duty is to arrest people named in warrants issued by the magistrates

Cossacks – Russian-inspired trousers, very loose fitting all round, and built for comfort rather than style

Covent Garden nun – a prostitute

Crew – a gang of criminals

Curricle – a smart, lightweight, two-wheeled, two-seated chariot drawn by two horses and designed for speed – the sports car of the Regency period

Dandy – a man who effects extreme elegance in clothes and manners

Deal porter – a worker who carries timber at the dockside

Drab – a nasty, sluttish prostitute

Drunk as an emperor – ten times as drunk as a lord, i.e. very drunk

Fichu – a kerchief worn by women to fill in the low neckline of a dress

Flush in the pocket – well off (usually temporarily)

Hackney coach – a vehicle for hire, with four wheels, two horses and six seats

Handywoman – a woman who helps at childbirth, an untrained midwife

Hatchet face – a long, thin face

Hue and cry – if a constable requires help in apprehending a criminal, he calls for assistance from all bystanders – this is known as raising the hue and cry

Inexpressibles – very tight (and therefore revealing) trousers or breeches

Instrument – the penis

Jarvey – a driver of a hackney coach

Kiddy – a young thief

Ladybird – a prostitute

Landau – a luxury city carriage with seats facing each other over a dropped footwell, and a soft top that could be folded back for full display of the occupants

Lighter – a flat-bottomed barge, used for transporting cargo between larger vessels and the shore

Lighterman – a man who pilots a lighter on the river

Lightskirt – a prostitute

Lorgnette – a pair of spectacles with, instead of arms, a single handle to hold them in place over the nose

Morocco – a soft, pliable goatskin leather traditionally used for bookbinding

Mother – (as in Mother Marwood) a female procuress, a keeper of a brothel

Noddy – foolish, simple

Ostler – a man who looks after the horses at an inn

Phaeton – a light four-wheeled carriage for two people, with open sides in front of the seat and front wheels smaller than the rear, and drawn by one or two horses

Priest-linked – married

Rake – a lewd and debauched man

Rum cove – a dexterous or clever rogue

Sand tray – a tray into which a wet document is placed, with sand then sprinkled over it to dry the ink

Size of ale – half a pint

Square toes – an old man, as they are fond of wearing comfortable shoes with room around the toes

Tom Cribb – world champion bare-knuckle boxer, winning his title in 1810 and retaining it in 1811 before retiring the next year to become first a coal merchant and later the publican of the Union Arms in Panton Street, near Leicester Square

Undress – for a Regency gentleman, to be in undress was to have removed his coat and cravat, which he would not do in polite or mixed company

Unlicked cub – a rude, uncouth young man

Upright man – the chief or principal of a crew of rogues

Waterman – originally watermen plied boats for hire on the Thames, but as hackney coaches took over as the main means of public transport in London, a compromise was reached to employ former watermen on coach stands around the city to provide water and care to the horses pulling the coaches – this is the role they fulfil in the 1820s

Wearing a wooden surcoat – in a coffin, i.e. dead

Thank you for reading this book. If you liked what you read, please would you leave a short review on the site where you purchased it, or recommend it to others? Reviews and recommendations are not only the highest compliment you can pay to an author; they also help other readers to make more informed choices about purchasing books.

ABOUT THE AUTHOR

Susan Grossey graduated from Cambridge University in 1987 and since then has made her living from crime. She advises financial institutions and others on money laundering – how to spot criminal money, and what to do about it. She has written many non-fiction books on the subject of money laundering, as well as contributing monthly articles to the leading trade magazine and maintaining a popular anti-money laundering blog.

Her first work of fiction was the inaugural book in the Sam Plank series, "Fatal Forgery". "The Man in the Canary Waistcoat" was her second novel, and "Worm in the Blossom" is her third. Four more Sam Plank mysteries are planned, to complete the series of seven.

Printed in Great Britain
by Amazon

40249095R00189